TE

JU

ALSO BY ELLEN WITTLINGER

Parrotfish

Blind Faith

Sandpiper

Heart on My Sleeve

Zigzag

The Long Night of Leo and Bree

Razzle

What's in a Name

Hard Love

FOR YOUNGER READERS

Gracie's Girl

Love & Lies

Marisol's Story

ELLEN WITTLINGER

Simon & Schuster Books for Young Readers
New York · London · Toronto · Sydney

ACKNOWLEDGMENTS

Grateful thanks to my editor, David Gale; his assistant, Alexandra Cooper; my agent, Ginger Knowlton; and Pat Lowery Collins, Anita Riggio, and Nancy Werlin for their help and advice on the manuscript.

Special thanks also to Patrice Kindl and to the Fine Arts Work Center in Provincetown, Massachusetts

SIMON & SCHUSTER BOOKS FOR YOUNG READERS · An imprint of Simon & Schuster Children's Publishing Division · 1230 Avenue of the Americas, New York, New York 10020 · This book is a work of fiction. Any references to historical events, real people, or real locales are used fictitiously. Other names, characters, places, and incidents are products of the author's imagination, and any resemblance to actual events or locales or persons, living or dead, is entirely coincidental. · Copyright © 2008 by Ellen Wittlinger · All rights reserved, including the right of reproduction in whole or in part in any form. · SIMON & SCHUSTER BOOKS FOR YOUNG READERS is a trademark of Simon & Schuster, Inc. · Book design by Alicia Mikles · The text for this book is set in AGaramond. · Manufactured in the United States of America · 10 9 8 7 6 5 4 3 2 1 · Library of Congress Cataloging-in-Publication Data · Wittlinger, Ellen. · Love & lies : Marisol's story / Ellen Wittlinger. —1st ed. · p. cm. · Sequel to: Hard love. · Summary: When Marisol, a self-confident eighteen-year-old lesbian, moves to Cambridge, Massachusetts, to work and try to write a novel, she falls under the spell of her beautiful but deceitful writing teacher, while also befriending a shy, vulnerable girl from Indiana. · ISBN-13: 978-1-4169-1623-9 · ISBN-10: 1-4169-1623-7 · [1. Lesbians—Fiction. 2. Authorship—Fiction. 3. Honesty—Fiction. · 4. Interpersonal relations—Fiction. 5. Homosexuality—Fiction. · 6. Cambridge (Mass.)—Fiction.] I. Title. II. Title: Love and lies. · PZ7.W78436Lu 2008 · [Fic]—dc22 · 2007018330

FIRST
EDITION

For my nieces:
Sarah, Emily, Meg, Lydia, and Louisa

"The truth will set you free.
But first it will piss you off."
—Gloria Steinem

CHAPTER ONE

I WOULD NEVER HAVE AGREED to room with Birdie
for the year if I'd known he intended to pick up every
stray that wandered across his path. The cat (which had
shown up on the fire escape) had already shredded my
favorite sweater, the puppy (from a box at the farmers' market) was a crotch sniffer, and I had put my foot down at the
first glimpse of that smelly ferret crossing the threshold. But
I was too dumbfounded to come up with an appropriate
response when he showed up with a lost human being.

I'd taken Noodles, the pug-poodle mutt, out to pee, so I
was already late for my shift at the Mug when Birdie appeared
in the doorway with a gorilla looming over his shoulder.

"Oh, great, you're still here!" Birdie said. "I wanted you to
meet my new friend, Damon. Damon, Marisol." He flipped
his hand between us. "Damon is in the theater department at
Emerson too!" Birdie exclaimed, as if it were miraculous that
he'd met someone from his own program. "Don't let Marisol
fool you," he continued. "She's small, but she bites."

Damon smiled nervously and extended a large paw in my
direction, but when I clasped it, there didn't seem to be much
life in it.

"Damon is brilliant," Birdie continued. "Oh my God, every word out of his mouth!"

There didn't seem to be all that many words *in* his mouth, but he was cute in a blushing, bearish sort of way, so I assumed "is brilliant" was Birdie's euphemism for "turns me on." *Whatever.*

"Listen, I'm late," I said. "I already peed the dog, but both animals need to be fed. I should be back around nine tonight."

"Okay," Birdie said. "We'll be here!"

We? I gave him a questioning look; he knew what I meant.

"You know, Marisol, living in a dorm is *so* hideous. We are really lucky we found this apartment in Somerville."

"Your mother found the apartment," I reminded him.

"You just don't know!" he continued. "I mean, you could get *anybody* for a roommate—it could be an absolute *abomination.*"

I waited impatiently.

"Poor Damon here lost the lottery. I mean *lost* it. He has been put into a room with a creature from the hellmouth; I am not kidding. You can smell him before you open the *door.*"

Damon nodded, then actually spoke. "He's a pig. He threw up in my shoes last night."

"That's too bad, Damon," I said. "I guess you'll have to put your shoes in the closet from now on."

"Well, the thing is," Birdie said, smiling at his new buddy, "I thought Damon could just move in here. And be *my* roommate!"

"*I'm* your roommate," I reminded him.

"There's plenty of room for three of us. Damon has a

futon, and you're out half the time at your job anyway, and we'll be in classes . . ."

I glanced at Damon, whose eyes now seemed slightly watery. Birdie sure could pick 'em.

"Damon, why don't you go make yourself some tea?" I suggested. "The kitchen is right through there, and the kettle is on the stove."

He nodded and left the room, hunching his shoulders just a little to fit through the kitchen doorway.

"I can tell you didn't meet *this* one at the gym," I whispered.

"Abs are not the only thing I look for in a man," he said, running a hand fondly over his own clothed six-pack.

"No? Pecs too? Biceps?"

"Marisol—"

"Birdie, if I wanted a bunch of roommates, *I'd* be in a dorm. Do you remember why I deferred college?"

"I know, you want to write, but—"

"I want to write *in this apartment*. Which is nice and quiet because there are only two of us in it. Which means, if you're not talking to me, nobody is."

He shook his head vigorously. "Damon is very quiet."

"How do you know? You just met him!"

"He hardly even speaks! Besides, he'll be in *my* room, not yours."

"Birdie, I can just barely stand having you and your two neurotic pets as roommates. Now you want to bring in some weird guy you hardly know?"

"He's not weird; he's just shy."

I peeked into the kitchen at Damon. He was backed up

against the refrigerator, staring in terror at Peaches, the pussy-cat, who was sniffing his flip-flops and fat toes.

"Who ever heard of a shy actor?" I said.

"He's not an actor. He's a director."

"I suppose he's gay and you like him?"

He tipped his head so his blond forelock fell into his eyes, and he grinned. "I'm not sure yet—of either thing. But I find him intriguing, don't you?"

"No, Birdie, I find him large and odd. And I don't want another roommate! This is a very small apartment. You should have asked me before you offered him sanctuary!"

Birdie wrinkled up his face in that stupid pout that has worked on his mother for the past eighteen years. But I am not his mother.

"I'll be back at nine o'clock. He better be gone," I said.

There were times I wasn't sure I'd made the right decision: taking this year off before going to college, moving in with Birdie, trying to write a novel between my tours of duty at the Mug and at my parents' house, reassuring them that deferring college for a year was not the first step toward receiving my bag lady certification. My high school friends had left for carefully chosen schools all across the country, but I felt like I needed this year off. Stanford University would still be there next year.

I'd gotten the idea when I went down to New York City after graduation to stay with June and her friends for a week. I'd met them in the spring at a zine convention in Provincetown on Cape Cod, that I'd gone to with my friend Gio. I liked June and Sarah and B. J., so when they invited me to go back to New York with them, I didn't hesitate. I was also trying to prove a point to Gio, which must have been successful, because I hadn't seen or heard from him in the four months since. I stayed in New York for a week and then went back for another week later in the summer. But it was a little problematic, because I knew June had a crush on me, and I didn't feel that way about her. By the end of the second week I figured I should just leave for good.

In the meantime, though, I'd met some of their New York friends, one of whom was Katherine, an editor for a large publishing house. June had showed her copies of my zines, and she seemed to actually like them. She gave me her card and said, "If you ever write a novel, send it to me."

A novel? Just like that the idea lodged in my brain and wouldn't go away. Suddenly the idea of starting college and taking Freshman Composition, Literature in Translation, and Existential Philosophy seemed like the most stultifying way I could imagine to spend the next year. It's not as if Katherine had made me any promises or anything. I wasn't doing it because I thought I'd get published. It just became the thing I most wanted to do. Just to be able to say, "I'm writing a novel." *I'm writing a novel!* Oh, my God. I wanted to be able to say that! I wanted to *do* it!

So I deferred my entrance to Stanford and moved from my parents' house into an apartment with Birdie. My father said that if I wanted to stand on my own two feet, I should see what that really meant, so I got a job pouring coffee and hustling cheeseburgers at the Mug in Harvard Square. As it turned out, waitressing at the Mug only allowed me to stand on one of my two feet, since rents in the whole Boston-Cambridge metropolitan area are higher than the Hubble Telescope. My mother, always a pushover, helped me to remain upright by stealthily contributing an extra couple hundred bucks a month to my survival fund.

And then it was September, and all the schools and colleges started up again. The Square was full of students buying books and meeting new friends. Actually, the whole city was full of students buying books and meeting new friends. Even Birdie wasn't immune to the excitement of it. I, however, was living with my best friend since sixth grade, twenty minutes away from the home I grew up in; I wasn't feeling the thrill.

Not that I didn't want to meet new people. In fact what I wanted more than anything—though I wouldn't have admitted it to anybody—was to meet a woman I could fall in love with. I'd been out and proud for almost two years, and the only love interest I'd had (if you don't count Gio, and I don't) was a girl who kissed me for a couple of weeks and then took off with the first guy who gave her a second look. That did a job on me—I got scared about trusting people, letting anybody know I liked them.

But I knew I had to get over that if I was ever going to have a girlfriend. My mother had this line about how "you have to kiss a lot of frogs before you find your prince." Or princess, in my case. I was eighteen years old, for God's sake. I had to put myself out there and start kissing frogs unless I wanted to be alone for the rest of my life.

So, I had two goals for the year: fall in love and write a novel. How hard could that be?

CHAPTER TWO

"HEY, YOU'RE LATE, MISS MARY-SOUL," Doug, the manager, said when I hurried in the door of the Mug. "I'm bussing tables here instead of counting up my morning receipts."

Or jawing with the customers. "Sorry," I said, grabbing a clean black apron from under the counter.

"I guess it took longer than you thought to put on all that makeup, huh?" I don't wear makeup. He chuckled at his own stupid joke.

"Roommate troubles," I said.

He held out his hand like a crossing guard. "Don't tell me about it."

"I wasn't going to."

"Everybody tells me their sob stories."

"Not me, Doug. I couldn't bear to see you sob."

"My roommate this, my landlord that, my husband, my wife—everybody's got a story." Doug shook his head.

"Yeah," I said, sticking change in my apron pocket. "People with lives are so inconsiderate."

Doug guffawed. "You kill me, kid; you kill me." Which was why I'd gotten the job. He appreciated somebody who could take his guff and give it right back.

The Mug was a Harvard Square institution, and Doug had been managing it since sometime soon after the Revolutionary War. It was apparently owned by a guy named Gus who was too old to even come in and drink coffee in a back booth anymore like he used to. It was a tiny place, only eight booths and half a dozen counter seats in all, but during peak hours there were often people standing in line in the doorway. Different kinds of people, but you knew they all had two things in common—you knew because they *told* you, over and over. They all missed the old Harvard Square, the way it used to be before the big record stores and clothing chains took it over, when there were lots of funky little places like the Mug. And they all loved Sophie Schifferdecker's pies.

Sophie had also worked at the Mug for a few centuries now, turning out hamburgers and tuna melts by the bucketload. In fact, as Doug liked to tell me, I was the first employee to be hired in the new millennium, even though we were now well into it.

"I don't hire young people anymore," Doug had said during my interview. "Too flighty. They work a few weeks, it's not as much fun as it looks like, and they take off on me."

Not as much fun as it looks like? That was really bad news.

"I promise to work for you for one year," I told him. "But then I'm going to college. And not around here."

"What's wrong with around here?" Doug had eyed me suspiciously.

"My parents live around here," I said. That was the first time I'd killed him.

Since the colleges had just started up again, the Square

was even busier than usual. Students weren't behind in their classes yet, so they had plenty of time to sit around and drink coffee while they got to know their new pals. One of the Harvard guidebooks mentioned the Mug as "the place T. S. Eliot probably spent his afternoons writing poetry and warming his hands on a hot cup of Earl Grey tea." Which you would think anyone would know was a load of crap, but every once in a while a few freshmen would come in, all wide-eyed, and order Earl Grey and grilled cheese sandwiches, and I knew from the way they looked reverently at the peeling wallpaper that they were impressed to have their hindquarters plopped in a booth where Great Literature may just possibly have been born.

Anyway, I ran back and forth between the kitchen and the booths for about two hours until the lunch rush was over. There was a short lull after I topped off everybody's coffee, rang up a few bills, and stuffed the tips in my pocket. I poured myself a cup of coffee and tried to decide whether to ask Sophie for a turkey sandwich or just go for a piece of pie. I was cutting myself a nice wedge of apple-blueberry when the bell over the door tinkled again.

I was not surprised, when I looked up, to see that it was her. A Harvard student—that was my guess—who'd come in alone every afternoon that week and burrowed into the corner booth, ordering tea and barely looking up from her book. Day after day she wore jeans and a plain white T-shirt, as if that were her uniform. She looked like she'd been raised in a convent, and not just because of her porcelain-pale skin either. There was also something so innocent about her, so

9

born-yesterday, it made me feel like I shouldn't look at her too closely. As if she wasn't fully formed yet, a chick just out of the egg, still damp and wobbly.

Except for ordering the tea, she didn't speak, which offended me slightly. The Mug was the kind of place where people yakked at you constantly, and even though that got on my nerves, this girl's I-am-so-smart-I-can't-be-bothered attitude was annoying me too. Where did she think she was? Au Bon Pain? I picked up my order pad and stalked over to her booth. If I had to put down my coffee, I was going to make it worth my while.

"So," I said, "you want some T. S. tea, and what else?"

She looked startled, her pale blue eyes open wide. "TST?" she asked. I guess she thought I was offering her drugs.

"Tea. You want tea, don't you?"

"Well, yes. I guess so."

"I mean, that's what you usually order, so I just assumed. How about a piece of pie with that?" I gave her my pushy-waitress smile.

She turned her book face down on the tabletop with a shaky hand. Grace Paley. *Enormous Changes at the Last Minute.* A book I'd always meant to read.

"Pie?" she whispered.

"Yeah, pie. It's a round pastry thing with fruit in the middle." I kept my pencil poised over the pad, waiting to write.

She blushed. "Okay, well, what kind do you have?"

"Today we have apple, blueberry, apple-blueberry, and pecan."

"I guess I'll have . . ." She seemed to be stumped.

10

Obviously she needed that Harvard education badly.

"Or, I could have Sophie make you a sandwich. Turkey, tuna, salami, grilled cheese—"

"I don't think—"

"Or maybe both, huh? Turkey sandwich? Blueberry pie?" I put the pad down on the table. She was going to order *something*.

"Do I—do I have to order food?" the girl asked. And when I looked at her again, her blue eyes were starting to swim.

God, I was such a bully. "No, you don't have to. You can just have your tea," I said, giving up.

She sat up straighter in the booth and managed to look me in the eye. "No, I would actually like a piece of pie. How much is the pecan?"

"It's a bargain at two fifty. The others are two bucks."

She thought it over. "Okay, I'll have a piece of apple pie."

I winked my smart-ass waitress wink. "Good choice. Everybody loves Sophie Schifferdecker's apple pie."

The girl nodded and picked up her book again. Just shy, I decided. Pitifully shy. Amazing she has the nerve to go out and sit in a restaurant by herself. I felt kind of bad about pushing her to order the pie. It occurred to me that she could be on scholarship—even at Harvard, not everybody was rich. I set the pie in front of her and decided not to get mad if she left me a crappy tip.

I sipped my coffee behind the counter and glanced at a copy of the *Boston Globe* that someone had left in a booth. I kept having the feeling that Pale Girl was looking at me, but

I didn't turn around to check. Then a bunch of customers came in and I forgot about her. Around four-thirty I realized she was still there.

"You want anything else?" I said, walking over to her booth. "More tea?"

She blushed. "Oh, no thanks. I guess I should leave."

I shrugged. "The dinner rush won't start for another hour—you can hang out, if you want to."

"Thanks." She ran her fingers through a headful of messy rusty curls.

"So," I said, "you a freshman?" Waitresses at the Mug are *supposed* to be nosy.

"A freshman? You think I'm a *freshman?*" She looked at me as if I'd slapped her.

"Hey, I'm just guessing. You're not?"

"No! I'm a senior."

I would never have thought that. "So, your last year at Harvard, huh?"

She blinked a few times. "I don't go to Harvard."

"Oh, sorry. It's just that a lot of the students who come in here do."

A light went on behind her eyes. "Oh, you thought I was a *Harvard* freshman! I get it. No, I'm in high school. I go to Cambridge Rindge and Latin."

"Really?" I sank down in the booth across from her without really realizing it. "We almost never get any high-school kids in here. They all hang out in the pit by the T station in nice weather, or at Bertucci's if they're hungry."

She shrugged. "Yeah. I'm new here. I don't know many kids."

"You had to change schools your senior year? That's rough. Did your parents move here for jobs or something?"

She smiled but didn't say anything for a minute. Obviously I was prying, which I normally don't do, but there was something kind of interesting about this girl, and I felt like I'd almost figured out the puzzle.

"My parents are still back in Indiana, where I grew up. I'm living with my older sister now. She went to Harvard, but she graduated last year. She works for an architect."

Pale Girl picked up her teacup and pretended to sip from it, though I knew the contents had disappeared a long time ago. What was she not saying? I looked at her clipped, unvarnished fingernails, the bashful smile that vanished as quickly as it appeared, her uniform of invisibility—were these clues?

And then I knew. Of course. That's why she'd been studying me all week. Why hadn't I seen it sooner? Was my gaydar on the fritz?

"Did your parents make you move out?" I asked.

She blushed again, knowing I'd figured it out. "Not exactly, but they were pretty upset about the whole thing, so my sister suggested I come out here and stay with her. It seemed like a good idea."

I nodded, hoping to keep her talking.

"I like it here pretty much—I mean the kids aren't mean to me or anything. I just don't know anybody very well. And Lindsay, my sister, doesn't get home from work until after six o'clock, and I hate sitting around her apartment by myself, you know? I mean, it's small, and it just doesn't feel like it belongs to me yet."

"So you decided to hang out here in the afternoon."

"I came in on Monday, and I saw you, and it seemed like . . . well, you know, I thought maybe—"

"That I was a lesbian too," I said.

She nodded.

"Well, I don't hide it. My name is Marisol," I said, sticking out my hand. "Marisol Guzman."

"Lee O'Brien," she said, hesitantly shaking my hand with only slightly more gusto than Damon the gorilla had a few hours before. We'd have to work on that.

"Welcome home, Lee O'Brien," I said.

It had taken me only moments to decide to befriend Lee. Maybe it was some latent social-worker instinct I'd picked up from my mother, I wasn't sure, but I was practically smacking my lips over the opportunity to help this baby dyke learn how to live in her new world. She needed somebody like me who was older (okay, only by a year), who'd been out longer (going on two), and was pretty much fearless about taking on the world (a trait I'd had forever, thank you very much).

It was only later, after Lee had hung around the Mug (eating a smuggled cheeseburger) until I finished work, and then followed me back to my apartment, where we'd walked in on Birdie and Damon howling over *Sex and the City* reruns and tossing popcorn kernels to the dog, that I wondered if picking up a stray of my own was such a good idea after all.

CHAPTER THREE

I WAS UNCHARACTERISTICALLY NERVOUS Saturday morning. Normally, I'm a little *over*confident—at least that's what my father says. He thinks it wouldn't hurt me to "have a little humility." It's not like I think I'm good at everything. It's just that when I *am* good at something, I'm *really* good at it. So, should I pretend not to be? I don't think so.

Anyway, I'd signed up for Writing Your First Novel, an eight-week Saturday morning course at the Cambridge Center for Adult Education, and this time I was sweating just a little bit. Could I actually write an entire novel? All I'd been able to do so far was jot down some ideas I thought might somehow hang together. Plus, I was likely to be the youngest person in the class. Usually adults took these courses, hence the name of the place, and I still didn't quite consider myself one of those.

The class met in a room in the colonial house on Brattle Street that had been home to the Center for decades. It had been dwarfed over the years by the mega buildings that surrounded it where posh chain stores sold expensive cookware and chic furniture, but like the Mug the house was a revered leftover from another era.

I arrived early because I couldn't sleep anyway; anger gives me insomnia. The night before, Damon had been monosyllabic as long as Lee was around (which was not long, as I was all talked out), but once she left and I went to bed, he crawled back out of his shell. He and Birdie were up half the night telling each other their entire life stories right outside my bedroom door. When I yelled at them to shut up, Birdie yelled back that he was sorry; then I heard him stage-whisper to Damon that I had PMS.

"With Marisol that means Pissy Mood Syndrome," he said, laughing.

"No," I shouted back. "It means Pass My Shotgun!"

But they were bonding, and nothing I said could stop them. When I got up at eight, after a few hours of restless sleep, they were passed out in the living room, Damon curled up on the ancient couch Birdie's mother had given us and Birdie spread out on the dirty red rug he'd rescued from a Dumpster. I banged around in the kitchen while I made coffee and toasted a bagel, but unfortunately they weren't disturbed.

The class didn't start until ten, so I got another coffee at the Mug and sat in a corner of the kitchen reading some Elizabeth Bishop poems while Sophie rolled out pie dough, her biceps bulging like Paul Bunyan's.

"Whatcha reading?" she asked. But when I told her I was reading poetry, she wrinkled her nose. "Too rich for my blood," she said, shaking her head. Whatever that meant.

I was getting fidgety by nine thirty, so I walked over to the Center to wait there. I was sort of hoping the teacher might arrive early, because brownnosing comes naturally to me, and I wouldn't have minded getting a jump on the other students. Not that I'm a grade grubber—these classes didn't give grades anyway. I just liked standing out from the crowd, which was usually not too difficult.

The course was being taught by somebody named Edward Deakins, who was listed in the catalog thus: *Edward Deakins has an MFA from Columbia University. He has three published novels:* The Mermaid's Stepson, Honk If You Love Me, *and* Fishing for Elephants in Tahiti.

I'd never heard of Edward Deakins or any of his books, but he'd published three novels, so I figured he must know something about how to write one.

As expected, I was the first student to arrive. There was a long rectangular table in the classroom, which made it impossible to sit in the front row, my usual ass-kissing choice. Edward Deakins might decide to sit at either end of the table, and if I chose wrong, I'd be far away from him. My only option seemed to be sitting in the middle of one of the long sides; at least that way I'd be close enough to catch his attention. I chose the side across from the doorway so I could make eye contact when he came in.

No sooner had I pulled my chair to the table than the second person arrived. I looked up, smiling (in case he looked teacherish) and ready to introduce myself. But that was not necessary, because the second person to arrive already knew me.

It was Gio, aka John Galardi, Jr., writer of the zine *Bananafish.* The guy who'd sought me out after reading my zine, *Escape Velocity*, and then asked me to his prom last spring so we could goof on it, or so I thought. The first boy (and I hoped the last) to say he loved me. Gio, whom I had not seen or spoken to in four months.

"What are you doing here?" he said, gawking at me from the doorway.

"Me? What are *you* doing here?" His hair was a little shorter than it had been, which made his dark eyes seem even bigger and deeper than they had before.

"I'm signed up for this class. I thought you'd be in California by now."

Of course he did. "I decided to defer Stanford for a year. I've got a job and I'm, well, I'm trying to write a novel."

He walked into the room then and took a seat across the table from me. "Really? You're writing a novel?"

"Aren't you? This is a novel-writing class."

"I know, but I just signed up for it because it was the only Saturday morning writing class they offered. You know, I like to have a reason to get out of my dad's apartment as early as possible."

"I remember." In truth I was really happy to see Gio again. I actually had this urge to run around the table and give him a big hug so he knew I wasn't mad at him anymore, but I was afraid he'd misconstrue things again. The last time I'd seen him it had seemed like friendship wasn't going to be an option, which was too bad, because we had a lot in common, Gio and me. Right down to the fact that the first person we'd each let ourselves fall in love with had hurt us badly. Unfortunately, I'd been the person who hurt Gio. So, even though it was totally not my fault, there was a tiny twinge of guilt working its way into my soul as I looked into his face.

"So, do you want me to drop the course?" he asked, his eyebrows knitting over his deep-set eyes.

"No, of course not. I mean, it's your right to be here as much as mine."

"I know, but if it's going to be too weird . . ." He looked away, not finishing the sentence.

I took a deep breath and blew it out, loudly. "Listen, I'm not mad at you. I was pretty freaked out after what happened last spring, but I'm not mad. I wish we could figure out a way to be friends again, but maybe you're still mad at me."

"I was never *mad* at you, Marisol. I was, you know . . . hurt." He looked away.

"I know, and I'm sorry about that. But you don't have to run away whenever you see me. I mean, we can talk to each other, can't we?"

He nodded. "I guess so. I'd like to. I miss having somebody to talk to about writing. That's mostly why I took this class."

I let a smile creep out. What the hell. "Me too. So, are you still writing *Bananafish*?"

"Oh, yeah. There's a new issue. How about you?"

I shook my head. "Not this summer. I've been working at the Mug and trying to come up with an idea for a novel. Have you kept up with that zine-writer girl from the Cape? What was her name, Diana something?"

Gio stared at me, trying, I thought, to figure out what my question meant. Like maybe I hoped he had a new girlfriend or something. Well, hell, he *should* have one—he was a good-looking guy, tall, dark, and skinny as a rock star—and it seemed to me Diana had fallen for him the minute she laid eyes on him.

"Diana Crabtree," he said, finally. "But she goes by Diana Tree."

"Oh, right, Diana Tree."

"I saw her a few times over the summer. She comes up to Boston now and then and spends the weekend with me at my dad's. But, you know, we're just friends."

I nodded. "Must make your Dad happy, though."

He laughed at that and so did I. I knew he was remembering the night we'd gone to an Ani DiFranco concert together, and then, because I'd missed the last train back to Cambridge, I'd spent the night at his dad's apartment, me in Gio's bed and Gio on the floor. We'd managed to have a really good conversation, and I felt close to him that night. Then the next morning his Dad assumed that I was his girlfriend and our sleepover had been something else entirely. It was pretty funny.

"Who knows what he thinks? My dad and I speak very little. He's still pissed off at me for not being his clone."

I nodded.

"What about you and . . . June?" he asked, looking down at the pen that was scribbling circles on the back cover of his notebook.

I shook my head. "Over," was all I said. This seemed like dangerous ground with Gio, talking about my love life, or lack of it. Besides, other students were starting to enter the room, and I didn't want them hearing any personal stuff. Gio shut up too, and we watched the rest of the class wander in. Or, as I thought of them, the competition.

As I'd suspected, everybody else was older. A few looked like college students, but most were real live grown-ups. The women all had big sack purses out of which they pulled new notebooks and pens. There were only two men (not counting Gio), and one of them was actually carrying a briefcase on a Saturday morning. The other guy, who was younger and had a flop of heavy blond hair in his eyes, made a big deal out of turning off his cell phone. One of the two college-age girls set up her laptop on the table and rested her wrists on the table in front of it, fingers at the ready, I supposed, to write the novel immediately.

And then *she* entered, looking around the table at each of us in turn. The way she carried herself as though she were striding onstage, the deliberate way she brushed the loose strands of hair out of her face (aware, I was sure, that every eye was on her), the decisive way she smacked her books down at the head of the table—this was someone who demanded attention and got it.

"As you can see, I am not Edward Deakins. A family emergency has forced Mr. Deakins to back out of his teaching commitments this semester. My name is Olivia Frost, and I think you'll find me to be a more than adequate replacement for Mr. Deakins. I'm a graduate of Harvard University and I've published short fiction in many well-respected literary magazines. I've taught for several years, and at the moment I'm finishing my own novel. Does anyone have any questions?"

I don't know if everybody else was staring at her the way I was, but I wouldn't be surprised. For one thing, she was stunning—the kind of beautiful you'd notice even if she were wearing a sweat suit and had her long dark hair stuffed up under a baseball cap. She had that high-cheekbone kind of beauty that just can't be hidden—not that she was trying to hide it. I have very little interest in fashion or clothes in general, but I couldn't help admiring the silky black pants and salmon-pink blouse Olivia Frost was wearing. Her clothes swirled around her body in a lovely way and more than hinted at what lay underneath. Large silver hoop earrings twinkled between the waves of her hair.

She sat carefully in her chair, crossed her legs, and looked around the table once more, not smiling, but taking us all in. When she got to me, I held my breath. Was I imagining it, or did her gaze stick on me just a second or two longer than it had on everybody else?

Suddenly I wished I'd spent more time on my hair—put in some of that new product I'd gotten to make the spikes stand up better. And I should have worn boots with heels. When you're as short as I am, you have to work at standing out.

"So, let's briefly go around the table, and you can tell me your name and why you want to write a novel."

The first woman swallowed nervously. "My name is Mandy, and, um, I'm not really sure I *can* write a novel, but I want to try. My mother wrote a novel once. She never got it published, but at least she did it."

Briefcase Man said, "I'm Steve Jeremiah. I'm a lawyer and

a lot of lawyers write novels, so I thought, why not me?"

The next woman sang out, "Cassandra Washington. I just *know* I can."

Mary Lou somebody was next—she was the one with her fingers already poised on the keys—then Heather and Amy and Michelle, all of whom had been English majors, so what the hell else were they supposed to do? Gio introduced himself as John, which was, of course, his real name, but there was no way I was ever going to be able to call him that. And finally there was the floppy-haired guy, who introduced himself as Hamilton Harper—though I realized immediately he would henceforth be Hamilton Hairdo to me—and said, "Since I sold my business last year, I've had a lot of time on my hands, so I figured, why not write a book?" Which seemed pretty obnoxious to me. Like, *Gee, I'm rich and I don't have anything better to do, so I think I'll be a concert pianist. I'm not busy, I might as well design a spaceship for NASA.*

And I could tell from the way he brushed his blond mop out of his eyes and smiled at Olivia that he thought he was good-looking too. I'm a confident person, so I recognize a fellow egotist, and my ardent hope was that this guy couldn't tell a pronoun from an adjective.

I introduced myself next, first name and last, then said, "I write all the time anyway—I've written a zine for two years now—so I figured I might as well try to write a novel."

Olivia Frost had a smile pasted on her face as if she'd heard all these stupid remarks before but would make an effort to teach us anyway. She launched into the subject.

"I don't expect anyone to finish writing a novel in eight

weeks' time—that would be ludicrous. What I hope to do is give you a foundation on which to build. We'll discuss character, plot, setting, structure, all the usual things, but we'll also feel free to break the rules. I'll give you exercises and assignments, and if you expect to get anything out of the course, you'll do them."

Briefcase Steve had his hand in the air. "Excuse me, Miss Frost, but if you haven't actually written a novel yet yourself—"

She cut him off. "You may call me Olivia, or, if you feel more comfortable being formal, *Ms.* Frost. I'm currently completing my first novel, which already has the interest of several publishers. Believe me, I know what you need to know. I also know what mistakes you're likely to make, and I can steer you away from the pitfalls. And I'm a hell of a good teacher. Any other questions?" Her glare must have been sending electrical shocks up and down old Steve's spine. He shook his head and shut up.

"First of all, let me say that the profession of book writing makes horse racing seem like a solid, stable business." There were a few muted laughs from the class. "If you are here because you believe that writing a novel will make you rich and famous, you ought not to waste your money. The only reason to write a novel is because you feel *passionate* about it, because you *must* write it."

She got up from her chair and walked behind us, circling the table, looking at no one. I swear I felt the heat when she passed in back of me, but I managed not to turn around. "Literature is the question minus the answer. Before you bother to put a word on the page, *know your questions.*" We scribbled that down in our notebooks, all of us, whatever it meant. The emphasis with which Olivia spoke made me feel as if every word out of her mouth was important, memorable, gospel truth. And it seemed I was not the only one who felt that way.

"If you know exactly what is going to happen in your book before you begin, you'll bore yourself and your audience. The suspense of a novel must be not only in the reader, but in the novelist. Surprise yourself and your audience will gasp too."

She continued to dispense gems, and we continued to hang on her every word. She talked about how you needed to know your characters' secret fears, hopes, and disappointments. "Even if you don't use that information in the book, knowing it will inform the characters and make them real." We did a few writing exercises to loosen ourselves up, and before I knew it, the two hours were over.

"For our next class," she said, "I want you to come up with two characters. They needn't be from your proposed novel—this is an exercise. Feel free to experiment. Tell me their names, their secrets, and what you already know about them. Then please write a short dialogue between them." A couple of people groaned at the assignment, as if they were in the sixth grade. Did they expect the novel to write itself? Did they think if they just showed up here for eight weeks, a book would magically appear before them with their name on it?

I took my time gathering up my single notebook and pen so that the rest of the class could funnel out ahead of me. Gio walked to the door and then turned back and leaned across the table.

He hesitated a minute and then said, "Any chance you want to grab lunch someplace?"

There was nothing I wanted more than to dissect the class (and Olivia Frost) with Gio. "Sure," I said. "Wait for me outside, okay?"

He nodded, then looked from me to Olivia, and walked out.

I didn't have anything particular to say to Olivia Frost, but early one-on-one contact with the instructor was always part of my teacher kiss-up routine, and in this case I was especially glad to pay my respects. Olivia seemed to be searching through her bag for something, but I had the feeling she might be stalling too, waiting for me.

"Hello," she said, as I came up beside her. "You're young to be in here, aren't you?"

"I'm not the youngest," I said, a little defensively. "The boy across the table from me is almost a year younger."

She smiled. "There's nothing wrong with being young. I was just surprised, that's all. A novel is a big undertaking. Teenagers usually start with something shorter."

How did she know I was still a teenager? Crap. She couldn't be that old herself—maybe twenty-three or twenty-four.

"I've written lots of shorter pieces. I think I'm ready to write a novel."

"Well, you would know better than anyone," she said, standing up. "What's your name again?"

"Marisol," I said. "Marisol Guzman."

"So, was there something you wanted to ask me, Marisol?"

"No, I just wanted to say I think this will be a great class. I already learned a lot just today." Hell, I sounded like some beginner who was just learning to suck up. I decided to go for it. "Actually, I do have a question. Do you think I could read your novel sometime? I mean I know it isn't finished yet, but—"

Olivia Frost threw her head back and laughed. "You don't waste any time, do you, Marisol?"

"It's just that I think I could learn a lot—"

But Olivia was shaking her head, her hair swirling. "I'm sorry, but I never let anyone read my work before it's completely finished. I'm superstitious that way."

"Oh, sure, I get that," I said. It had been a long shot, but at least now she wouldn't forget who Marisol Guzman was. "Well, anyway, the class was great."

Olivia smiled and placed a pearly-white fingernail on my sleeve. "I hope you'll continue to enjoy it."

"I'm sure I will," I said as I backed away, tucking her glorious smile in my memory and wondering if there was the slightest possibility that Olivia Frost could be gay.

CHAPTER FOUR

GIO AND I HAD JUST ORDERED LUNCH at the Bombay Club. It was a little pricey for somebody who worked at the Mug, but it was my favorite restaurant in the Square, and I was in such a great mood after class that I didn't want to dilute it with lesser cuisine.

"Thank God that Deakins guy bailed out. She's brilliant, don't you think?" I asked Gio.

"I guess."

"You *guess*?"

"I mean, she's interesting and smart and certainly beautiful, but there's something about her that bugs me. She's too good to be true. And just a little condescending, didn't you think?"

"Of course she's condescending—she's *too good to be true*! She's probably used to people being kind of dull in comparison to her."

"Oh, come on. A lot of people are smart—we're sitting in Harvard Square. *You're* smart, and you don't act like you're better than the rest of us." A grin struggled to lift one corner of his mouth. "Well, not all the time."

I decided to ignore that. "If a woman is smart *and*

gorgeous, like Olivia, she probably has to act that way or she'll be deluged with admirers."

He narrowed his eyes at me. "You really think she's that great?"

I sighed. "Were you in the *room* this morning?"

"Obviously not in the same room *you* were in," he shot back.

It was fun having Gio to banter with again. There was nothing I liked better than a worthy opponent—which he was—and it seemed like we might be able to get our pugilistic footing back. The whole morning had raised my spirits greatly, and when our food arrived, mango chicken curry with a side order of samosas, we both dug in hungrily.

After a few moments of chowing down, Gio said, "So I guess that means you think Olivia Frost is beautiful."

I stopped chewing. "You *don't*?"

He shrugged. "I guess she is. Just not my type."

"Probably not. I think she might be *my* type," I said.

Gio seemed stumped for a minute, then got it. "You mean, you think she's a lesbian?"

I shrugged. "Not a hundred percent sure, but it seemed to me there was something a little flirtatious about the smile she just gave me."

"You mean after class when you were sucking up to her?"

"No, I mean after class when I was introducing her to her new favorite student."

The waiter came back to refill our water glasses. Gio waited for him to leave, then said, "She didn't *look* very gay."

He knew before I said anything that he'd stepped in shit. "Okay, I know there is no one way that gay people *look*. Except

29

that sometimes you can tell right away—don't deny it."

"Yeah, if the person *wants* everybody to know, you can tell; if not, you can't."

"Fine. So, I'm just saying, she wasn't advertising it."

I dipped a samosa in sauce and bit off a crispy chunk. "I can't believe you didn't like her."

"I'm not saying I didn't like her. I think she'll probably be a good teacher. I wrote down a lot of the stuff she said."

"I wrote down every word that came out of her mouth," I said.

He nodded. "Well, it's possible I did too."

We stopped talking for a few minutes to savor the curry and look out the big second-floor windows at the crowd hurrying along the sidewalk. I think we both noticed the pink blouse at the same moment, and that long dark hair swishing from side to side like a L'Oréal commercial. A warm flush ran through my body and no doubt manifested itself on my cheeks, which I could feel glowing.

"There goes the professor," Gio said, still looking at her and not me. "Going into Starbucks to refuel after a long morning of dazzling the masses."

"She's got a laptop with her. I bet she writes in there."

Gio shook his head and turned back to his lunch. "I never understood how people could work out in public like that. It seems so show-offy."

I kept looking at the coffee shop door through which she'd disappeared. "'Show-offy' is not a word. Besides, writing is a lonely occupation. Some people need the stimulation of being in a public place to write—there's nothing wrong with that."

"Maybe. But noon on Saturday at Starbucks? That place is busier than Fenway Park right now. I could never work with all that noise."

"Well, not everybody is like you, Gio."

I kept looking out the window until I realized Gio was watching me watch the Starbucks door. "Any sign of her?" he said.

My cheeks warmed again. "No." I forked up some chicken and forced my gaze to remain inside the restaurant. "I was just thinking that I never see anybody writing at the Mug. Even though it has that whole T. S. Eliot thing going for it."

"I bet it doesn't have Wi-Fi, though," Gio said.

"Well, that's true, but you don't need Internet access to write."

"Are you kidding? When you're stuck, you gotta go check your e-mail!"

"I just play Solitaire. Seriously, the four months I've worked at the Mug wouldn't you think I'd have seen *somebody* hanging around writing? It's more atmospheric than Starbucks. I think it's weird."

"Maybe you could start a trend."

"That would mean spending more time there than I already do. Which could happen if Birdie becomes any more annoying to live with than he already is."

"I remember Birdie. You live with him? How did that happen?"

"Just because you and Birdie didn't hit it off doesn't mean there's something wrong with him. He's been my best friend since forever. It's just that he keeps picking up homeless puppies on the sidewalk, and the latest one is a two-hundred pound guy. I am not amused."

Gio sat back in his chair and sipped his tea. "Not a little jealous, are we?"

"Of those two? I don't think so." I could see that it might sound like that, but I wasn't. *And I would really not be jealous at all if only I had a girlfriend!*

Gio let the topic drop. After a minute he got up to go to the bathroom, and while he was gone I indulged my desire to stare out the window. Olivia might have left already, of course, but surely I would have caught a glimpse of that pink blouse out of the corner of my eye. Somehow I felt she was still inside, working intently.

When Gio got back, we divided the bill and paid the waiter. Out on the street I had to forcibly plant my eyes on Gio so they wouldn't drift across the street.

"Well," Gio said, looking a little uncomfortable, like he had when he'd first walked into the classroom and seen me sitting there. "I should get going. I want to check out a couple of used-book stores in downtown Boston this afternoon."

"Right. I guess I'll go home and try to do some writing this afternoon. I work the six to midnight shift at the Mug tonight."

"You could get a cup of coffee at Starbucks first," he said, testing a smile.

I narrowed my eyes and gave him a soft punch on the arm. "You think you're so smart, don't you?" Our eyes met and he looked away.

"Okay," he said, and the discomfort level multiplied between the two of us. We'd been fine at lunch, but saying good-bye is awkward when you don't know what you mean to the other person, or what you're allowed to mean to them. "So, I'll see you next week."

"Yes, you will," I said. Then, as he finally turned to leave, I called him back. "Gio?" Feeling reckless, I ran up and gave him a hug. "I'm really glad to see you again."

His shoulder muscles tightened under my grip, and he did not return the hug. He pulled his head back and looked at me.

"I'm glad to see you again too, Marisol. But, you know, things are still kind of . . . weird. I mean, maybe you shouldn't . . . do this."

I leaped back as if he'd told me he had bird flu or something.

"Right! Sorry! I didn't mean—"

"I know what you didn't mean; that's why I don't think you should touch me. At least not now. Not right away. I'm still kind of susceptible—"

"Sure. I got it," I said, nodding vigorously. "You're right. Duh, I'm dumb."

"I just don't want to . . . I was so screwed up last spring. I don't want to feel like that again." He couldn't look at me.

"Yeah, of course. Anyway, okay, see you later!" I waved at him and turned around, walking in a direction I didn't want to go, away from Starbucks and the possibility of seeing Olivia Frost, because I couldn't let him see me chasing her like that. Crap. How could I have forgotten how loaded a touch was to Gio? I was wrecking everything again. *Get away from him,* I said to myself. *Get away fast.*

CHAPTER FIVE

L UCKILY, BIRDIE WAS OUT when I got home, and he'd taken the dog, too, so the place was as quiet as it was likely to get. On the T coming back to the apartment I'd decided to file Gio's unsettling good-bye into some nether portion of my brain to be dealt with later. It was a technique I'd had success with before; sometimes I seemed to lose the most disturbing files altogether. If I was going to get any writing done that afternoon, I'd have to access the excitement I'd felt in Olivia Frost's class. I told myself that if anybody could write a novel in eight weeks, surely it was gifted-and-talented me.

Olivia had said to find the names for the characters in the exercise first. They should be names that had resonance for the writer and were meaningful in some subtle way the reader might pick up on too. I'd been sitting across from a young Hispanic mother on the train, and I'd watched her tuck a blanket around her sleeping baby—tenderly, but also efficiently, as though she'd been doing this sort of thing for more than just a few months. She gave me the idea for my two characters and what they might be talking about. They weren't the characters I wanted to write a novel about—but I didn't know who those characters were yet or what the novel was going to be about. I thought maybe doing the exercise would help me figure that out.

So, I decided that one character would be based on my mother—my adoptive mother, Helen, that is. And the other would be based on my biological mother, whom I'd never met and about whom I knew little except that she was Puerto Rican and had been a teenager when I was born. For a while I'd written long letters to her, even though there was no place to send them. It was just a way of making her up in my mind and talking to her. I hadn't written a letter to her in months, but because I'd thought about her for so long, I was pretty sure I could come up with something for her to say.

The name I decided to use for my adoptive mother in the exercise was Dorothy, for obvious reasons. Birdie had called her that behind her back for years because of her out-of-fashion bowl-shaped haircut, which had been made famous by some Olympic figure skater named Dorothy Hamill back in the Dark Ages. I also liked the allusion to that girl lost in Oz, not that I intended to do some big analogy with tin men and scarecrows or anything. It was more that my mother, raised to be a socialite but never fulfilling that shallow promise, had always seemed a little bit lost, too, not quite at home anyplace. The name Dorothy was just significant enough.

I had no idea what to name my unknown mother. I didn't know her real name; my adoptive mom had never met her, and the records were sealed until I turned twenty-one. Of course, I'd always wondered what she was like, so I wanted a name that would encompass my imaginings. I had an old book of baby names that I'd taken from my mother's office when Birdie was trying to come up with monikers for his new pets. It was so ragged it had probably been around since before my own birth. In the back there were lists of names popular in other languages. I went to the Hispanic pages and made a list of possibilities.

Alida
Amelia
Beatriz
Betina
Carmen
Catalina
Cecilia
Chela
Evita
Genoveva
Graciana
Juanita
Lolita
Lucita
Luz
Margarita
Martina
Mercedes
Nuela
Paloma
Rosita

Sofia

Solana

Trella

Ynez

Ysabel

I stared at the list. Which name defined the woman I imagined? Probably not Paloma or Lolita, much as I liked the associations they carried. The teenager who handed me over to a nurse was probably not wearing bright red lipstick and flirting with every old guy in sight. At least that was not the way I thought of her. I crossed those names off the list.

Evita wouldn't work either, as its associations were already too strong. I liked the *M* names a lot, but they also seemed to have confusing connections. Margarita was that tasty lime drink Mom made in the summertime; Martina was the lesbian tennis player; Mercedes was the übercar my Yankee grandparents drove to the country club where they played tennis and drank Margaritas.

Sofia sounded beautiful, but soft—surely, my mother would not be soft. Luz, I knew, meant light in Spanish. Was that the association I wanted? Not really. When I imagined my mother, she stood in the shadows, partly hidden. And she was probably more dark than light. After all, she'd given away her child.

The name I kept coming back to was Carmen. It sounded like caramel, that smooth brown sweetness so perfect with a tart apple. I knew there was also a famous opera by that name, but I didn't know anything about it, so I went online to do some research. It turned out that in the original story of *Carmen*, the heroine was a Gypsy girl killed by her jealous lover. The beautiful, mysterious woman loved her freedom and would not commit to any one man, even though it meant her death. I was definitely on the right track here for exotic mother material.

So, Carmen and Dorothy were my characters. This naming stuff was fun.

Now for their secrets. Of course, I thought I knew most of my mother's secrets, which I supposed would be Dorothy's, too. Her unhappiness with the social world she grew up in. Her rift with her parents when she married Dad. Her disappointment at not being able to have children of her own. The miracle, at age forty-two, of having a Puerto Rican infant deposited into her arms for safekeeping. Mom had never been shy about telling me these tales, and I felt certain I could bring to life the character of forty-two-year-old Dorothy based on what I knew.

The harder character to imagine was Carmen. I decided, first of all, to make her eighteen, my age, an age at which I could not even imagine having a child to raise. We were alike in that way, young Carmen and me. But who was she really, besides a pregnant teenager, very likely without many resources, maybe without a man or even a mother to help her out? Who was my Carmen? I took some notes on the possibilities.

I had discarded several false starts on a conversation between the two when I heard a key turning in the lock. Damn, he was back.

"Hello!" Birdie shouted. "Are you home?" Noodles started barking and pushed open the door to my room with her nose, then padded in.

"Hey, Noody," I said. "Did your lazy daddy finally take you for a walk?" I had to admit the pooch was pretty sweet, although the size of her feet seemed to be an omen that the poodle part of the combo planned to overshadow the pug part, and in the future Noodles the puggle would require even more space in the apartment than she did now.

"We're back!" Birdie said, sticking his head into my room. "Are you working?"

"I *was*," I said pointedly.

"Well, since you're stopped now anyway, would you mind giving us a hand carrying some of Damon's stuff up here?" He squinted his eyes and smiled his I-know-I'm-a-bad-boy smile.

"*What?*"

Birdie slipped through the door and closed it behind him. "Shhh! I don't want him to think you don't want him here."

"I *don't* want him here. I told you that." Noodles leaped onto my lap and knocked two pens and a notebook to the floor.

"Marisol, he doesn't have any choice. His roommate is terrible!"

"Of course he has a choice. He can complain to someone at the college. He can dump the roommate's stuff out in the hall. He can trade roommates. He can get his *own* apartment. Whatever. But he cannot live here!"

The patented pout. "But I like him. And we're just getting to be friends. If you let him stay, he'll help me walk the dog."

"You mean, he'll help *me* walk the dog, don't you?"

"And he'll pay a third of the rent and the utilities—that'll help out!"

"Your mother pays your half," I complained. I knew I shouldn't start arguing with Birdie—it showed weakness, and he would take advantage of it.

"But it'll help *you*!" he said. "You can barely squeak by on your Mug salary and what Helen slips you on the side."

"Birdie, why do you like this guy so much?"

"Are you kidding? He's adorable!"

"He's weird. He's afraid of the cat. And he hardly even speaks to me."

"That's your fault—you haven't made any effort with him. Besides, I thought you didn't want him to talk to you— it would disturb your genius-at-work thing." Birdie picked up my thesaurus in one hand to use as a weight for his bicep curls. His other arm reached for my bedside table lamp.

"Stop! You're not in the gym, Mr. Universe. That lamp is breakable."

Reluctantly, he set it back down. "Anyway, Damon is a dog person. I know he doesn't say much, but I like him. His hair is so touchable, and he's bigger than me. He's definitely got possibilities."

"And maybe cooties, too," I said, giving up in disgust.

Birdie laughed, knowing he'd won. "I'm gonna fix up this teddy bear. Just you wait and see. In two weeks' time even you'll think he's adorable."

I put Noodles on the floor and picked up the stuff that had fallen. "He better be the most adorable person I've ever met, because if he's not, he's out, Birdie. You got that? *Out.*"

"Oh, I'm sure he'll be out *very* soon," he said, giving me a knowing smile. "Now, just give us a hand with the futon, and then you can go back to being Ernest Hemingway or Virginia Woolf or whoever you are."

I don't know why, but Birdie can talk me into things I would never allow anybody else to. I went downstairs with the two of them, and we hauled and dragged and pulled the heaviest futon on earth up three flights of stairs, wedged it into Birdie's room between his bureau and a wall of CDs, and then collapsed on it.

"That was hard," Damon said, breathing heavily, "even with your muscles, Superman."

Birdie flexed a bicep. "Don't blame me. You two weren't holding up your end."

Damon reached over and caressed Birdie's arm. "My God, how did you *get* those arms?"

"Lifting weights," he said, rolling back his T-shirt sleeve to show off the other one too.

"Dumbbells," I said. "Isn't that what they're called?"

"I don't care what they're called," Damon whispered to Birdie. "They're amazing!"

"They're yours," Birdie whispered back.

Bad enough I had to break my back lifting the cement-filled futon of my new, unwanted roommate into my apartment, but now I was being subjected to this inane flirting on top of it. It was too much. I deserved a lover more than Birdie did. Yes, I was jealous. It wasn't fair that I was going to have to listen to their squirrelly lovespeak all the time when I—who was so ready—should be the one beginning a great new romance. It was *my turn*.

I left the boys to stare into each other's eyes, or test the futon, or whatever came next for them. The first line of my novel was starting to race around in circles in my brain, and I ran to my desk to get it down on paper.

Christina had always believed she was born lucky—smart, funny, and just good-looking enough to get pretty much everything she wanted, except, of course, the thing she longed for most: love.

CHAPTER SIX

ARVARD SQUARE KEPT LATE HOURS, especially in September, when everybody was still pumped about starting the new school year. The booths at the Mug were all full at eleven o'clock, so when Lee came in, she slid onto a stool at the counter.

I shot her a smile over a tray of pies I was busy delivering around the room. "Hey," I said. "You're out late."

She shrugged and waited for me to get back behind the counter. "I went to a movie at the Brattle," she said.

"What did you see?"

"*Cat on a Hot Tin Roof.* They're having a Tennessee Williams film festival. Last week I saw *A Streetcar Named Desire.*"

"Really? I've never seen either of those. They always seemed like they'd be so testosterone-soaked," I said. "Marlon Brando in a ripped undershirt."

"Oh, they're much more than that—they're Tennessee *Williams!*" she said. "Nobody writes like him!"

"I guess." I was unconvinced. "My school put on *The Glass Menagerie* a few years ago. It seemed a little silly, with the sister who was afraid of her shadow, and that shrieking mother."

Lee stared at me in abject disappointment—like Noodles when you ate in front of her and didn't share.

"Although," I said, "maybe it was just because this awful girl was playing the mother. Probably if I saw a better performance of it—"

"You would!" Lee said. "Oh, you'd love it. I mean, you're a writer—you'd have to love it!"

Typically, the hair stands up on the back of my neck when somebody tells me what I *have* to love, but I couldn't get mad at this foundling.

"If they show the movie of *Glass Menagerie*, maybe we could go see it!" she said, bouncing on her heels.

"Maybe." But not likely. The women in those stories were always half nuts and pining away for somebody—not good role models for Lee in her present state. I poured hot water over a tea bag and did not look at her puppy eyes.

"You hungry?" I asked her. "Sophie made a lemon meringue pie before she left, and nobody's touched it. It's so good. When I was a kid I called it cloud pie or sky pie and made my mom get it for my birthday instead of a cake."

"Sure," she said, squeezing out a smile. "I had some nasty frozen stuff from my sister's freezer for dinner. Left over from the Ice Age."

I cut Lee a big piece of sky pie and set it before her with a flourish. The crowd was starting to empty their pockets onto the tabletops and leave, so I cut a piece of pie for myself, too, and poured a cup of coffee. "So, what have you been doing all day? Weather is so great this time of the year I just want to be outside."

She shrugged. "I slept late. Had lunch with my sister and her boyfriend at some Chinese place. They had plans for the afternoon, so I pretended I had homework to do. Took a book and sat down by the river for a while."

"I love it down by the river. You know, next weekend is the Cambridge Arts Festival all along the riverfront. People making and selling art, music groups, theater groups, jugglers, fire eaters . . . a little bit of everything. It's fun. You should go." It occurred to me that a nicer person would have said "we" should go. But that would have made it seem like I was asking her on a date or something, and I didn't want to give her the wrong idea. I mean, it was fine to hang out with her, but she was kind of new to the game, and she might think I was giving her signals when I wasn't. This time I was choosing the girl, not letting her choose me.

She nodded and sighed. "Maybe I will," she said without much enthusiasm. She wasn't scarfing down Sophie's pie the way I would have expected, either.

I leaned over the counter so she'd have to look at me. "What's wrong? You aren't deciding to flee back to Indiana, are you?"

"No, although I do think about it. I mean, I like it here—it's pretty and there's lots going on—but it's so different from where I grew up. It's *too* pretty or something. It seems like everybody is rich and smart and perfect. That whole Harvard thing. How do you ever feel like you belong here? If you're not part of it, I mean."

I didn't have an answer for that one.

"I guess you *are* part of it, so you wouldn't know," Lee said.

I'd really never thought of Cambridge as someplace you belonged or didn't belong. It was just my home. "I've never lived anyplace else," I said.

"Do your parents work at Harvard?"

"No, my mother is a psychotherapist, and my Dad teaches at MIT."

She smiled. "MIT—same difference. You're a dyed-in-the-wool Cambridge brat, aren't you?"

I shoveled in a big chunk of lemon filling. "Let's just say this wouldn't be the first time I've been called a brat."

Lee sipped her tea and bounced her fork off the meringue.

"So, do you miss your parents?" I asked.

She shrugged. "I don't miss all the craziness that's been going on since I came out to them. But, yeah, I guess I do miss them. We were always pretty close . . . before. And I miss my best friend, Allison. I could tell she was freaked out, even though she said she wasn't. It's not like I had a crush on *her* or anything—which I told her—but she hasn't even e-mailed me since I've been here. It's like Indiana has disappeared off the face of the earth. Or I have."

"That sucks. You must be close to your sister, though. I mean, she wanted you to come out here and live with her."

"Yeah, that was a surprise too. I mean, I'm nothing like Lindsay—I never was. She's really pretty and obviously smart enough to get into Harvard—always had a million friends, while I had, well, Allison. Lindsay's a really hard worker, and I've always been kind of lazy, which drove her nuts. But I guess she feels sorry for me now. The gay thing doesn't bother her, though—she says it explains me."

"What does she mean by that?"

"Like, why I've always been kind of quiet, why I never joined stuff or spoke up in classes or made myself visible in high school, like she did."

"Does it?"

"Partly, but I've never been as outgoing as Lindsay anyway. And I don't like the way everything I do now, she assumes it's because I'm gay. Like, 'Oh, you're wearing cargo pants? I guess that's because you're a lesbian.' Or, 'You're a vegetarian now? I guess that's because you're a lesbian.' 'You're reading a book by a woman? I guess that's because . . .' God! It's just stupid. It's like being gay is my entire definition now—it's the only thing I'm allowed to be. And I hate that!"

Interesting. Had that happened to me? I thought it probably had, but that I just didn't mind it as much as Lee did. I was about to respond to her when Doug came in to get the night's receipts. He was prowling around in back of me, not happy that I was yakking to a friend.

"You started checking out yet?" he asked me. Obviously, I hadn't.

"Those two tables haven't paid yet," I said.

"Well, you can get a start on it, can't you? I want to get out of here quick tonight." He grumbled and banged open the cash drawer.

There were open tables now, so I nodded to Lee. "I'm done at midnight if you want to wait over there for me." She slid off the stool and slunk over to a table. I felt bad having to brush her off when she was in the middle of her big story about feeling out of place, but what could I do?

"You want me to do that?" I asked Doug. He was tallying the credit card slips and writing numbers in his book.

"I got it," he grumbled. "Get those tables wiped down and refill the salts, peppers, and ketchups."

He wasn't usually this grouchy, at least not with me. "There a problem?" I asked him.

He grunted. "I wanna finish up here so I can get back to the hospital."

"Is somebody sick?" I didn't think Doug had any family.

"Gus is in the hospital. Heart trouble."

"Gus? You mean *the* Gus? Who owns the place?"

"Who else would I mean?" he barked as he flipped up the levers that held the bills in place in the drawer. "Nobody around anymore to help him out but me."

"Gee, that's too bad. I hope he'll be okay."

"He's eighty years old, and his ticker's wore out. One of these days he'll be gone . . . and this place will disappear with him." He glanced up. "Pay attention—that table's ready to leave."

I couldn't tell if Doug was upset about Gus being sick or just annoyed that he had to go back to the hospital so late at night. I knew he was a creature of habit; any change of schedule irritated him, so it could be just that. But maybe he and the mysterious Gus were friends. It would make sense after all these years. And was he just being overly dramatic about the Mug having to close if Gus died? Surely somebody would take it over and keep it going.

"How long have you been working for Gus?" I asked.

"Long enough to know that you have to refill the salts,

peppers, and ketchups every damn night!" he bellowed.

"Okay!" I yelled back. Nothing pissed me off more than being yelled at unfairly.

The last table of paying customers headed for the door as I grabbed a rag to swab down the tables. Lee was huddled in a booth slimed with coffee and spilled cream. She moved her elbows so I could wipe it clean.

"I could never work for somebody who yells like that," she whispered.

"He's okay," I said. "Just in a bad mood tonight."

"He's staring at me. I'll wait outside, okay?" She slid out of the booth and scurried to the door.

"You don't have to," I called, but she was halfway out the door already. "I'll be out in twenty minutes."

I rounded up the salt and pepper shakers from the tables. "Thanks for scaring off my friend," I said to Doug, hoping he'd lose count of his ones.

"Eighteen, nineteen, twenty . . . Next time get yourself a friend who ain't such a scaredy-cat." He banded the twenty ones and went on counting.

I finished up my closing duties and threw my apron in the laundry bag.

"You on tomorrow?" Doug asked.

"Not till Monday afternoon. I hope Gus is okay."

Doug nodded and kept on counting. I'd never seen him look so morose before. I guessed even if your friend was eighty it was still hard to think of him dying.

Lee was waiting for me in the pit by the T stop. There were a bunch of skateboarders and skanky-looking high school girls hanging out there too, making too much noise for my present mood.

"Let's go sit down there," I said, pointing to the concrete triangle in front of a row of shops on Brattle Street. During the early evening there were usually street performers out there, doing magic or mime or something of interest to tourists and five-year-olds. But this late at night there were only a few couples scattered around, sitting on the walls talking.

Lee pulled a pack of sugar-free gum out of her pocket. "Want some?"

"I don't chew gum—it goes bad too fast and then you have to figure out where to spit it out."

She nodded. "I know. It's a nervous thing for me. Better than smoking, though."

"That's for sure."

She ran her hand through her messy curls again, obviously another nervous habit. "Listen, I'm sorry I was telling you all about my stupid life back there. I mean, it's not like I've got it so bad or anything. I know that."

"I don't mind listening. But I have to warn you, I'm one of those people who tend to want to fix things. You know, don't just bitch about it; change it."

"Right," she said. "You're right. So tell me what you did today."

I smiled. "You mean tell you how a *perfect* day is spent by a local brat in Harvard Square? Well, I worked as a waitress in a greasy spoon from six to midnight, and got yelled at by my boss for no reason at all—"

"Which didn't actually bother you that much."

"True."

"What else? What did you do this morning?"

"Oh, I went to a class at the Cambridge Center for Adult Education—a class on writing a novel."

Her eyes opened wide. "Really? You're writing a novel?"

"I'm trying to. That's why I didn't go right to college this year. The teacher is this unbelievable woman named Olivia Frost. She's brilliant. She went to Harvard."

She shrugged. "Not so impressed by Harvard; my sister went there, you know."

"Well, sister, schmister, I'm telling you—Olivia is brilliant. Listening to her talk is mesmerizing. I spent the afternoon working on the writing exercise for next week, and then I started working on the actual novel. She's got me really psyched about it."

Lee shook her head and laughed. "Your life *is* perfect, Marisol. Do you even realize that?"

"Oh, shut up and give me a piece of gum already."

Maybe I wanted Lee to think my life was perfect, that no improvements were necessary. If she thought it was true, maybe I would too. Until I went home by myself and realized that, like my alter ego, Christina, I was still missing one thing.

CHAPTER SEVEN

I DID SOME MORE WORK on the character of Christina during the next few days; I figured out her background, her age, and where she lived, all of which seemed to be embarrassingly similar to my own statistics. But I knew that first novels were often that way, especially when the author was young. Hey, I hadn't had that much life experience yet— I had to write about what I knew, didn't I? I changed a few things: She lived in Boston instead of Cambridge, and she worked as a receptionist for a dentist because I thought I could get a few tooth jokes out of that. But Christina was an eighteen-year-old lesbian, and she lived with her gay best friend, and her mother was the president of the local PFLAG chapter (Parents and Friends of Lesbians and Gays), because those are some of the things that make me the way I am, and I wanted to be able to use them in the novel.

Since Christina's parents were less wealthy than my own, she was attending college part-time and working for the dentist part-time. She was smart and cocky and a little bit of a wiseass. And of course her fatal flaw was her desperate wish to be loved. This was going to get her into trouble down the line, although I wasn't sure yet just how that would happen.

I was stumped about who she would fall in love with. No one as unrealistic as Olivia, I told myself, because things like that just didn't happen.

When the writing stalled, I daydreamed about Olivia. I couldn't help it. She was parked right there in my unconscious, just waiting to materialize in all her long-legged beauty. One night I got out the phone book and looked up FROST, OLIVIA, and there she was! She lived in Somerville too, but on the other end of town from me. I wrote her phone number and address on a piece of paper and stared at it as though there were secrets to be divined from the letters and numbers. Thank goodness neither Birdie nor I had a car, or I would have driven over there and parked outside her house for the chance to see her come and go. I knew that rational people called this stalking, but I was beginning to realize that when it came to Olivia, I was not particularly rational.

It was just as well that I had plans for Wednesday night. Mom had said to come for dinner and to bring Birdie, and Birdie had called her back to see if it would be okay to bring Damon along as well. Of course Mom said yes, unaware that Damon was a big termite eating away at the foundation of my long friendship with Birdie.

Yes, I am opinionated. Yes, there are people who would say I'm difficult to get along with. And yes, I did take a rather immediate and perhaps irrational dislike to Damon on first meeting. But once it became clear that this person was really moving into my space whether I liked it or not, I made an effort. I spent Saturday night watching season-one *Will and Grace* DVDs with both of them and didn't even make any cracks about how in reality nobody would be able to stand living with either Will *or* Grace because they both whined too damn much.

On Sunday morning I made blueberry pancakes, not realizing, of course, that Damon didn't eat blueberries because "the texture is just . . ."—and here he made a gagging noise. Thank you very much. So I made an entirely new batch *without* blueberries, and Birdie wanted to know if I didn't think they were "a little gluey." I did not say, "The better to paste both your mouths shut."

When Damon complained to Birdie that my music had awakened him from a Sunday afternoon nap, and Birdie complained to me about it, and then Damon begged me to forget all about it, really, it was no big deal, and Birdie gave him a big wet smack on the cheek and me a look of disappointment—after all this I did not scream in their faces about the night they'd kept me awake yakking and playing seventies disco music in the living room!

I was being a goddamn saint about all this because Birdie had been my best friend, my main confidante, since I was ten years old. He didn't always get me, and I didn't always get him, but we didn't judge each other for our idiosyncrasies either. We'd nursed each other through a couple of rocky romances, and he could always make me laugh. Until now. Now he apparently made Damon laugh, but the humor of the situation was going right over my head.

I knew this seemed like pure jealousy on my part, but it wasn't the so-called romance I begrudged him—it was the fact that it was being conducted *in my apartment.* That wasn't the deal. I was happy to discuss Birdie's boyfriends with him over my morning coffee; I just didn't feel like sharing breakfast with the actual boyfriend. Especially one who was afraid of me and the cat in equal proportion.

I did manage to get Birdie alone for a few minutes on Wednesday morning when he conned Damon into taking the dog for a walk.

"So, I guess you and Damon are a couple now? He's gay?"

Birdie was picking his way across his bedroom floor, choosing clothes from piles that all looked equally dirty and stuffing them into a laundry bag. "Well, bi, anyway. He doesn't like labels."

"But you're a couple, right?"

Birdie squirmed. "Sort of."

"What does that mean?"

He sniffed at the armpit of a white T-shirt, then threw it back on the floor. Will Truman would not approve. "Well, we're a couple here, at home. But not necessarily at school. I mean, we don't flaunt it."

Birdie had been flaunting it since before puberty. "So, Damon can't quite get the old closet door open, huh?"

"That's not it! I told you, he's bi. Besides, that closet metaphor is getting tired, don't you think? Old homos have that closet issue, but we've grown past it."

"Oh, have we? You young homos are free to be you and me?"

He gave me the finger. "Damon doesn't want homosexuality to define him. There's nothing wrong with that."

Huh. That was what Lee had said too. It was an issue I hadn't thought about before, but I could see their point. You wanted people to see you as a person first. You didn't always want to lead with your sexuality.

"Look, Birdie, I'm just trying to point out that throwing yourself at someone who won't admit he likes you doesn't make for a healthy relationship."

He propped one hand on his hip and sneered at me. "You should talk. You're the one who keeps getting yourself mixed up with totally inappropriate people."

"What?" I hated when he turned an argument back on me, and hated it especially when he was right.

"First you were crazy about that girl Kelly, who wasn't even a lesbian—"

"I didn't know that, did I?"

"And then you spent every weekend last spring running around with what's-his-name, that straight guy who had a big crush on you."

"Gio. Again, not my fault. As far as I was concerned we were just friends."

"Seemed to me you felt awfully guilty about something that was not your fault."

I didn't have a good answer for that, so I switched topics. "That's not your T-shirt. You're putting Damon's clothes into that bag too. What, are you doing his laundry now? Are you *married*?"

Birdie threw his head back in disgust. "God, Marisol, will you please go get yourself a girlfriend already and get off my back!"

Dad wasn't home from work yet when we arrived Wednesday evening. Mom was helping Ellie, their cook and housekeeper, with dinner—or possibly just getting in her way. She paused long enough to give each of us one of her patented hugs (which sometimes feel more like mugging than hugging). Damon saw it coming and tried to get away, but it was no use—Mom is an expert at corralling wayward calves. His eyes bulged as though she were squeezing the life out of him instead of the love into him.

"I'm so glad you brought your new roommate, Marisol."

"He's really more Birdie's roommate than mine," I said.

Mom figured out what that meant in no time. "Oh, how nice, Birdie! I'm thrilled for you both—you make a lovely couple!" As the newly elected president of the local chapter of PFLAG, there was nothing Mom liked better than being included in all the homosexual news. Damon's jaw dropped and his face went pale—I made a wild guess that his mother was not as blithe about such things as mine.

"Thanks, Helen," Birdie said as he raided the fridge for the Dr Pepper my mother kept on hand just for him. He handed one to Damon and opened one himself. "Anybody else want anything while I'm in here?"

I shook my head.

"Your father's going to be a little late," Mom said. "He had some papers that had to be graded by tomorrow."

One of his favorite excuses. After all, how could you call him on it? A professor had to grade papers, didn't he? Not that I thought he wasn't grading papers, just that it could take him a long time to accomplish the task if he was in no hurry to get home. Birdie had always made Dad a little uncomfort-able, but since our coming-out duet, Dad couldn't seem to handle Birdie at all. For an old guy Dad is still pretty macho. Once, Birdie came over in a pink tank top that showed off his cock-a-doodle-do tattoo (two roosters with their wings around each other), and Dad was quietly apoplectic, his eyes roaming the room for someplace to land that wasn't Birdie's shoulder. He knows that Birdie and I are both gay, but he doesn't like to talk about it, and he'd rather not be forced to think about what it actually means.

Dad still wasn't home by the time we sat down at the table.

"So, Damon," Mom said, "I hear that you're at Emerson College with Birdie."

"Yes, ma'am," Damon said, forking through his risotto as though searching for blueberries, or some other gag-worthy ingredient.

"Studying acting, too?"

"No, I want to be a director. A stage director."

"Lots of those jobs going begging," I said.

"Yeah, he should be a *novelist*," Birdie said. "You can never have too many of those."

"Where are you from originally, Damon?" Mom continued.

"Um, I was born in California, but we moved around a lot while I was growing up because of my dad's job. The rest of my family is in Michigan now."

"Michigan!" Mom said, as though it were some tropical paradise she longed to visit. "That's a beautiful state, isn't it?"

Damon shrugged. "I guess so. I haven't seen that much of it."

"Do you have brothers and sisters still at home?"

He nodded. "One of each. They're thirteen and fifteen."

"How lovely! Are they homosexual too?" she asked brightly.

At the look of shock on Damon's face, Birdie squirted Dr Pepper out his nose.

"Well, they haven't *said* they are," Damon finally responded.

"I only ask because some studies say that it runs in families, but I don't know that there's any hard evidence for it yet. Do your parents mind?"

"Mind that I'm gay? We haven't actually talked about it. I mean, I think they suspect that I might be . . . going in that direction."

"If you'd like me to speak to them, I'd be happy to," Mom said. "I've often advocated for young people who—"

Finally, Birdie interrupted her. "Helen, Damon is bisexual. At the moment."

"Well, isn't that wonderful!" my wacky mother announced.

Dad was bustling in by then. "Hello, sorry I'm late." He crossed to my chair and gave me a brisk cheek kiss, the only kind I'd ever gotten from him. "Hello, Birdie. Glad you could all come," he said, without actually looking at either Birdie or Damon. "What have I missed?"

"Not much," I said. "Mom was just about to ask Damon for the details of his bisexuality."

Dad and Damon both took on a greenish pallor.

"I was not!" Mom said. "Marisol, you're terrible!"

"She is, Helen," Birdie agreed. "Our girl is very bitter these days. Methinks she needs to find herself a girlfriend."

59

"Methinks you're an idiot," I said, lobbing a green bean at his forehead.

Mom leaned over and put a hand on my arm. "Have you been meeting any new people, honey?"

"Not really." Not anybody I'd mention to *this* crowd.

"When you go to college, you will," she assured me. "That's practically what college is *for!*"

"College is for learning!" Dad said huffily, banging his plate a little bit. "Not for meeting people. I don't intend to pay a fortune for my daughter to *meet* people."

"Well, of course it's for learning," Mom said in her calming voice. "But it's also for socialization. Marisol will adore college!"

"I've made some great friends already," Damon said, smiling.

"You see? Damon *loves* college!"

"Mom, you don't have to worry," I assured her. "I'm going to college, eventually."

"Of course you are, sweetheart. I know that. And when you get there, you'll find yourself a lovely girlfriend."

"I hope you're right, Helen," Birdie said, giving me a sad look. "If anyone will have her." Fortunately, he was sitting across from me so I could kick him in the shin.

"I'm not paying forty thousand dollars a year for you to find a—a—a girlfriend!" Dad sputtered.

"Oh, Raphael, don't be silly," Mom said, shushing him with a finger to her lips.

Birdie, who had always been just a little nervous around my blustery father, fidgeted in his seat. "This is the *best* risotto, isn't it, Damon? I'm going to have to get this recipe!"

Damon the finicky, who'd basically just moved the risotto around on his plate until half of it spilled over onto the table-cloth, nodded enthusiastically and said, "It's fantastic!"

Dad did not try to hide the rolling of his eyes.

CHAPTER EIGHT

BY FRIDAY MORNING I STILL HADN'T GOTTEN very far with my idea for the dialogue exercise. I couldn't go to class the next morning unprepared, and I was getting frustrated. The boys didn't have classes on Fridays, so Damon was running lines with Birdie for Birdie's first college play, which was some goofy thing by Molière. Birdie was practicing tripping over his own feet, and both of them were squealing with laughter like two little pigs. Finally, I packed up my laptop and headed to the Square. Any place was quieter than my apartment.

The Mug wasn't too crowded in the daytime, but the idea of writing there all afternoon and then waiting tables there all night was not appealing. I pretended not to know where I was headed, but it was just a game. *She probably won't be here anyway,* I thought as I stepped through the door at Starbucks.

Still, I could barely breathe as I glanced surreptitiously around the room. I was right: no Olivia. But there was an empty table in the back near the window, so I grabbed it before even getting my first cup of coffee. For a few minutes I felt self-conscious sitting there staring at my laptop screen, but the allure of working in public became apparent to me quickly. Even though I was surrounded by people, no one paid the slightest bit of attention to me. There were so many conversations going on that they became a pleasant buzz of white noise that didn't interrupt me at all. I liked the fact that people all around me were busy; it helped overcome the blank-page (or blank-screen) phenomenon of writing down those first words. It almost seemed like I was carrying on a conversation with the rest of the world.

I let Carmen and Dorothy run around in my head and just be with each other. Before long they were speaking, speaking so fast that I could barely keep up with them. It was breathtaking to write like that, full speed ahead without even stopping to edit or reread.

By the time Olivia showed up, I'd forgotten why I'd gone there in the first place.

"Well, hey!" she said, coming up to my table. "Do you come here to write too? I thought this table had my name on it."

I looked up into her wide smile and gasped. Even if you have an active fantasy life, it's still shocking when your dream walks in the door, shining its perfect teeth at you.

"Hi! You can join me—there's room here!"

"Oh, I don't want to interrupt you," she said.

"No, you wouldn't be!" I said, taking my shoes off the other chair and moving my bag to make room for her. "I'd like the company."

"If you're sure," she said, settling herself in. "I do love to work in here, don't you?"

"It's my first time," I admitted, "but yeah, I like having all the talking around me."

She nodded and sat down. "I have to be drenched in words, literally soaked in them, before the right ones form themselves into the proper pattern at the right moment."

I loved the way she put things; it was what I'd been thinking, but I could never have said it like that.

"So, have you finished the exercise for class?" she asked.

"That's what I'm working on now. I did some other writing this week, though—just ideas, really, for my novel."

"Wonderful!"

"Your class last week was inspirational." I knew I sounded like the worst brownnoser alive, but I actually meant it this time.

"Was it?" she said with a little grin. "Well, I hope I can continue to live up to my own high standards."

I knew she was tweaking me, and I was embarrassed. Could she tell I had a big old crush on her? I probably wasn't the first student to find her "inspirational."

"Well, don't let me keep you from working," I said.

"Oh, you won't," Olivia said, brushing her luxurious hair out of her eyes. "Nothing stops me. Even when the screen is blank, I have the miraculous feeling of the words being there, written in invisible ink and waiting for me to make them visible."

"You do? That's amazing. I wish that would happen to me."

"It will someday, when you've written as much as I have." She opened her laptop and her attention immediately disappeared into it, leaving me to search for my own invisible ink.

Fortunately, I'd just about finished the exercise, because having Olivia sitting across the small table from me was torturously distracting. She contemplated the computer screen and tapped out words on the keyboard without an obvious thought for me, her foolishly smitten student, sitting so close and unable to think about anything but her. Half an hour before I really had to be at the Mug, I closed my laptop and told Olivia I was leaving for work.

She looked up from her writing, dreamily. "I hope you got some work done."

I nodded.

"Good. See you tomorrow, huh?"

"Absolutely."

In order to get from the table to the front door I had to think consciously about how to walk. It wasn't until the fresh air slapped me in the face that I began to clear my head of the aura of Olivia.

When I got to the classroom the next morning, Olivia was already there. She looked up and gave me a quick wink, which discombobulated me so much I could barely manage to find an empty seat. For fear of giving away my feelings I didn't dare look up at her until she started to talk to the whole class. I gave Gio a little wave—he was at the other end of the table—and wondered if he could tell I'd been whacked in the head with the love stick.

We started right off reading our exercises out loud. I wanted to wait to read my piece until last, if possible, so I could calm down a little bit first. Lots of people volunteered to go ahead of me, either because they wanted to get it over with or because they were so proud of what they'd written.

Some of the character dialogues were pretty bad, I thought. A couple of people—Steve Briefcase for one—didn't even get the rhythm of how you wrote dialogue. It was as if they'd never read a novel before, or even listened to people speaking. Mary Lou wrote a pretty interesting piece about a young couple who were discussing whether or not to get married, and I wondered how true to life it might be. Hamilton Hairdo read this ridiculous thing about two Labrador retrievers discussing their idiotic owners—I was completely thrilled by his incompetence (and a tad annoyed that Olivia smiled at him, as if she found something about the piece amusing). Gio had written a conversation between a boy and his mother. I knew it was pretty close to home from the things he'd told me about his mother last spring. As always with Gio the writing was good, but he shied away from the emotional part of it.

Olivia said something nice to everybody, then gave some gentle critiques, focusing mainly on style and how to make dialogue sound realistic. She recommended we read our work out loud to see if the dialogue sounded like real speech—which I did anyway—and she explained that after this week she expected us to critique each other's work too.

I couldn't concentrate on what she was saying because I was distracted by the way she looked. If I'd thought she was beautiful before, it was because I hadn't realized how truly amazing she *could* look. It was a very warm day, and Olivia had prepared for it by wearing a white sundress that fell just below her knees. It was a simple dress that showed off her tan, well-muscled arms and legs; she wore nothing else except white sandals and the large silver earrings. Her black hair was piled on top of her head with a few wisps falling down against her cheekbones. Talk about dramatic looks. I could tell I wasn't the only gobsmacked fan; when Steve Briefcase tried to form a sentence, he made the mistake of looking up at her, and his words slipped and stumbled all over each other. Olivia Frost was the definition of stunning.

And then it was my turn to read, which I attempted to do with confidence.

The first time Dorothy saw Carmen was in the waiting room of the San Juan hospital. A social worker introduced them.

"*Mucho gusto, señora*," Dorothy said.

"I can speak English," Carmen said. "I'm not stupid."

"I'm sorry!" Dorothy said, putting her hand over her mouth. "I didn't think you were stupid. I just thought..."

"I'll leave you two alone to get to know each other," the social worker said before she disappeared into the crowded hallway.

Dorothy sat down next to the very pregnant teenager whose child she hoped to be able to adopt after it was born. Dorothy was a therapist; she spoke to people in all sorts of difficult situations all day long, but now she couldn't seem to think of a thing to say to this girl, Carmen. And Carmen obviously wasn't going to speak to her first.

"So," Dorothy finally said. "How far along are you?"

"Thirty-six weeks. You won't have to wait long." Carmen sounded angry.

"Oh, I wasn't asking for that reason! I just wondered." Dorothy wished the social worker hadn't left so quickly. "I'm very grateful to you for this, Carmen. My husband and I have tried for a long time to have a child of our own, but we haven't been successful. I promise you I will be the best mother I can be to your baby." Dorothy laid a hand on Carmen's arm, but the young woman pulled herself away from the touch.

"How old are you?" Carmen wanted to know.

"I'm almost forty-two," Dorothy said.

"That's old," Carmen replied.

"Well, some women my age do get pregnant, but the doctor says I won't be one of them."

"I am eighteen," Carmen said, lifting her head proudly.

"I know."

"Why do you so much want a baby?" Carmen asked. "They are a lot of trouble. I have two younger brothers. They cry and whine and are always hungry."

"Oh, but they also laugh and hug you. And you can teach them things—how to walk and talk and read. I think it would be the most exciting thing I've ever done!"

Carmen made a face. "Your life must not be very exciting then."

"Well, I guess it isn't." Dorothy said, laughing.

"Are you laughing at me?" Carmen wanted to know. "I cannot stand for people to laugh at me."

"At you? Of course not! I'm laughing at myself," Dorothy said.

Carmen was quiet a minute and then said, "Well, that's okay then. If you laugh at yourself before other people can do it, it surprises them."

"I think you're right," Dorothy said.

"Will you make sure that nobody ever laughs at my baby?" Carmen asked.

"Carmen, I promise you that."

After I'd read my dialogue aloud, I looked at Gio first, without even thinking about it. He gave me a thumbs-up and a smile. I smiled back, and then Olivia spoke and the rest of the world disappeared.

"Marisol, that is a wonderful piece of work," she said, her black eyes sparkling into mine. "I am *so* impressed that a writer your age can get to the heart of her characters like this. I could feel the anger in Carmen, the resentment against this older woman who plans to take her baby away. Her mixed emotions. And Dorothy also elicits our sympathy. She doesn't know what to say; she doesn't want to offend. Their emotions are so clear—great job!"

She went on for a few minutes about the difficulties of writing dialogue that reflects the characters' emotions, saying she hoped everyone could see how expertly I'd managed to do this. She finished with, "You've really taken this assignment to heart. I can't wait to see what you do next!" The rest of the class was staring at me with bald emotions ranging from awe to envy to downright resentment. But who cared?

I couldn't speak, couldn't drag my eyes away from her face. Olivia's response to my work had been completely positive. To no one else had she given such enormous praise, and I believed I deserved every word of it.

Once our dialogues had all been read and commented upon, Olivia gave her lecture for the day. I took out my notebook and, like the week before, made notes on all she said. How I did this, I'm not sure, because I could barely hear the words. There was a kind of buzzing in my ears, or maybe around my whole head, and I felt as if I were watching the class proceeding from someplace far outside of it. I had been elevated from these mortal surroundings to some more exalted sphere by the admiration of Olivia Frost, and I hoped to remain in that bubble for a long time.

Eventually I managed to come to my senses enough to get down the assignment for the following week: to describe a place we knew well. Olivia begged us to give not merely the kind of description a tourist brochure might—no warm, sunny beaches or quaint little cottages or majestic mountains. She hoped we would search more deeply for our sense of place and find the way in which the setting gave additional meaning to the story. She left us with this thought: "It is the function of art to renew our perception. What we are familiar with we cease to see. The writer shakes up the familiar scene, and as if by magic we see a new meaning in it."

Gio waited for me by the door after class. "Wow, she really loved your dialogue!"

I glanced back at Olivia, but she was surrounded by the English majors, and Mr. Hairdo was waiting his turn too. "I know," I said. "I'm kind of amazed."

We headed for the outside door. "It *was* really good—the best one of all. I bet you *will* write a novel this year."

I basked in the additional praise. "I hope so. I mean, that's why I took this time off."

Gio pushed the door open, and there, sitting on a bench reading a book and twirling her hair around her finger, was Diana Tree. He was obviously not surprised.

"Hey!" he called.

She bounded toward us like a lanky colt. "Hey! Hi, Marisol! Wow, I'm so glad to see you again. I couldn't believe you and Gio were taking the same class."

It was strange seeing her again. I knew she must know all about what happened between Gio and me last spring—she'd been there for some of it. And I'd known, even then—anybody with eyes could have seen—that she had a crush on the boy herself, which made it pretty likely that she wasn't actually all that happy to see me again. But she was one of those people who just don't have any meanness in them, or much of a protective coating, either, and I had no intention of getting in her way or screwing up whatever might be going on between her and Gio. Even if it meant dragging myself down out of the clouds of conceit and acting like a regular human being.

"Hi, Diana," I said. "Good to see you, too. Are you here for the weekend?"

"Yeah. There's this Arts Festival thing going on this weekend, and Gio thought I'd like to go to it."

"Right. Down at the river. I was thinking of going too." I realized too late what Diana would feel she had to say then.

Her smile drooped just a tiny bit, but she pushed it back into place. "Oh, do you want to come with us? We were going to get something to eat first and then—"

Think fast. "Thanks, but I can't. I promised to meet a friend of mine . . ." I gestured vaguely into the distance as if there were an actual meeting place where my imaginary friend waited impatiently. I didn't like lying to her, but in this case it really was for her own good.

"Marisol just knocked it out of the park in class," Gio told Diana. "She read this incredible piece, and now the teacher is in *love* with her." He was kidding, but I knew my face flushed anyway.

"No surprise. You're such a good writer," Diana said.

"Thanks." I glanced at my watch. "I really should get going. Maybe we'll run into each other later at the festival."

"Good!" Diana said. They both waved and wandered off in the direction of the river—not, I noticed, touching each other in any way. *Damn, Gio, get a clue.* I began to walk purposely in the opposite direction, but then realized there was nothing I wanted over there, so I just ducked into a doorway until they were out of sight. Now what? I had been thinking the lunch-with-Gio thing might be a regular occurrence, and I was disappointed, not only because I couldn't continue to wallow in my classroom victory, but also because I enjoyed talking to the guy as much as I ever had. Could we really not be friends just because he'd once declared his inappropriate love for my lesbian self?

I was back in front of the Center for Adult Education again, trying to decide what to do with the rest of the day— grab a slice of pizza at Bertucci's, slink down to the festival and hope I didn't run into the zinesters again, or just go home and work on the assignment—when Olivia Frost slipped through the door of the Center, her white sandals slapping lightly against her heels.

"Just the person I was hoping to run into!" she said, smiling.

CHAPTER NINE

SHE DIDN'T EXACTLY ASK ME to have lunch with her; she just said she was starving and didn't I love Café Algiers, which was her favorite restaurant in the Square, and before I knew it, there I was, once again sitting across a tiny table from Olivia Frost.

"I know it's hot," she said, gathering her skirt above her knees and fanning her long legs with it, "but I have to have my coffee. Do you like espresso?"

"I do," I said, "except those tiny cups don't last long enough."

She laughed. "Well, then, we'll just have to order two or three right off the bat. Coffee is the blood in my veins."

Just the idea that she *had* blood and veins and other human organs made my own circulatory system pound in my ears.

She leaned across the table and pointed to the menu. "Tell me, do you like hummus? They make the best hummus here I've ever tasted."

I wasn't a particular fan of hummus, but I was in the mood to be tutored by Olivia Frost in all things. "I'll try it," I said.

She laid a long-fingered hand over my small, scruffy knuckles and said, "Something tells me you aren't always this agreeable."

I wasn't making this up, was I? There was something going on here. "Why do you think that?" I asked.

She lifted her hand and sat back in her chair to appraise me. "Because you're smart. You think for yourself. You're a little scornful of some of the other people in the class."

"How do you know—"

"By the look on your face when you're listening to them. You're used to being the star, aren't you?"

"I wouldn't say that . . . exactly." But she gave me a knowing smirk, and I had to laugh. I had a feeling this was a case of it-takes-one-to-know-one. "I guess that's true sometimes."

"Well, you're definitely the star in my class. I can tell already. And someday, when the rest of the world knows you're a star too, maybe you'll look back and remember that I was your first real teacher."

Okay, she'd only heard one thing I'd ever written, and it was two pages long. Besides, teachers didn't usually tell you this kind of stuff until the class was over, so you couldn't lord it over anybody else, or slack off on your work because, duh, you were the *star*. There was definitely something unteacher-like going on here, and, even though my ego was big enough to file this kind of flattery in one corner and still have plenty of room to dance, her praise was making me a little dizzy.

"Thanks. How long have you been teaching?" I asked, to get the focus off myself.

She rolled her eyes and laughed. "Seems like forever. I love teaching. I was born to teach."

"Where else do you teach?"

"At Harvard."

"Really?"

She shrugged. "It's not as good a gig as it sounds. The students all think they know more than I do. It's exhausting. I prefer teaching adult education. Those people appreciate a good teacher."

I nodded, wondering if I was one of "those people."

"You're not the usual adult ed student. Why aren't you in college?"

"I deferred Stanford for a year so I could write a novel."

Olivia almost did a spit-take with her coffee. "You plan to write a novel *before* you go to Stanford? I knew you had balls when I first saw you."

No matter how good-looking she was, that irritated me a little. "I don't think it takes *balls* to write a novel."

She laughed. "Okay, then, chutzpah. Nerve. Ambition. It does take all of those, and I suspect you've got them in spades."

A waiter came around then, and Olivia ordered for both of us, which gave me a chance to sit back and look at her. She had the waiter under her spell immediately as she cocked her head and flirted. Maybe that was all she was doing with me, too, adding me to her life list. If so, I wasn't complaining. After all, flirtation was the way things got started, right? Not that I'd had much practice using my own latent seduction skills, but I figured there was no better time to begin.

Over lunch we talked about our families. I explained the origin of my Carmen and Dorothy story, which she seemed to find fascinating. Then Olivia told me about growing up in the suburbs of St. Louis and waiting impatiently to go to college on the East Coast, where she felt all intellectual life was being lived.

"I was so alienated from my family and their friends—there didn't seem to be anybody else like me back there. Or anybody like you, for that matter. I felt so isolated—I longed for a larger life. I could practically taste it!" She leaned forward as she spoke, and it seemed as if we were alone in the café—no, alone on the planet. The way you feel when you really click with somebody.

I leaned in too and said, "I liked the hummus." Clearly, flirtation did not come naturally to me, but Olivia laughed and squeezed my hand.

She insisted on paying the bill and then said she planned to go down to the Arts Festival at the river for a little while, and did I want to come with her? The farthest thing from my mind was Gio and Diana—my earlier conversation with them had been erased by the hour with Olivia—so I happily agreed.

On the walk down we spoke again about writing a novel.

"You know what you have going for you, don't you?" Olivia asked me.

"Ah, no, but I hope you'll tell me."

"The worst enemy of creativity is self-doubt. But you're so confident—that will make all the difference." Her arm gently surrounded my shoulders. "I wish I'd had your confidence at your age."

The back of my neck prickled as her hand grazed it, but I tried to remain calm. Could my pathetic attempt at banter actually be working? "Well, you aren't exactly ancient, are you?"

She laughed. "Not exactly. How old do you think I am?"

I shrugged. "I don't know. Twenty-five?"

She smiled her perfect, lipsticked smile. "Twenty-eight."

"So, ten years older than me."

"A decade. A lifetime, at your age," she said wistfully, retracting her arm.

I dared to lean against her and whisper, "Yes, but I'm very mature for my years, you know."

"I'm sure," she said. "And you're kind of adorable, too."

Adorable? No one had ever called me *that* before. I looked fully into Olivia's eyes for the first time, daring myself to hold them until hers gave way, but she'd had more practice. My eyes fell into hers, my equilibrium completely destroyed, and I had to look away in order not to swerve into a building.

We turned the corner onto Memorial Drive, which was blocked off to traffic for the Arts Festival. There were a lot of skaters, skateboarders, and bicyclists to dodge, so we crossed immediately to the grassy strip along the river where the artists had set up their booths. A girl with a fiddle was fronting a scruffy bluegrass band, and we stopped to listen for a minute while I tried to control my wildly beating heart.

Without speaking we wandered through a few booths hung with watercolor landscapes and monotonous pictures of boats. The craft booths were better, and I managed to get my mind on something other than the nearness of Olivia's body. Several potters were displaying beautiful pieces, and I contemplated getting a few mugs for the apartment. But they weren't cheap, and if Damon broke one, I'd have to kill him, thus severing my relationship with Birdie for good.

Olivia found something she liked at a jewelry booth. She

was holding earrings that looked like clumps of grapes to her lobes. "Do you like these?"

"On you, sure."

"But not on you?"

I shook my head. "I don't wear much jewelry. It gets in my way."

She put a hand on her hip. "When you're digging ditches? Or fixing the plumbing? Come here. These would look great on you." She held a pair of green enameled leaves to the sides of my head, her fingers brushing my ears.

"Oh, no," I said, backing away. "Way too . . . green. And leafy."

"Not an environmentalist, huh?" She put them down. "Are there any here you like? Lesbians are allowed to wear jewelry, you know."

Her gaydar was in working order, but it rattled me a little that she would say that so nonchalantly. Was she making an announcement, or just commenting on my obvious interest in her?

"I know that," I said, not looking up. I scanned the rows of earrings, but there were none I could imagine wearing. Also on the table lay rows of pendants, most of them strung on silky black cords. One caught my eye immediately: a polished amber stone—the colors swirling from gold to copper to a rich auburn—inlaid in a plain silver setting. It was like a meditation stone, something you could hold in your hand and contemplate for hours. I picked it up and it felt good in my hand, just heavy enough.

"Oh, that's lovely," Olivia said. "I can see you wearing that."

I looked at the price tag. Forty-five bucks. Not terribly expensive for a spoiled brat, but way too much for a part-time novelist and coffee shop waitress.

"I don't think so," I said, laying it back on the table reluctantly.

"But you love it! I can tell!"

"It's kind of expensive. I can live without it. Besides, it would look better on you than me." For a brief moment I toyed with the idea of the coffee shop waitress buying the beautiful necklace for her beloved teacher, but realized immediately how sketchy *that* would look.

We walked away from the booth, but Olivia kept looking back as if she thought the pendant might follow me, its rightful owner. After a few more booths, we found an empty bench near the water, in sight of the fire jugglers.

"You know what? I'm just going to run back and get those grape earrings after all," Olivia said. "Won't take me a minute. Wait here?"

I was happy to sit down and have a minute to myself to think about what was going on. But no sooner was Olivia out of sight than I saw Gio and Diana coming my way. *Crapola.*

"You did come!" Diana said. "Where's your friend?"

"She's . . . um, looking at jewelry."

Diana perched on the bench next to me and Gio sat down next to her.

"Did you hear that band down by the bridge?" he asked. "They're called Girlyman—they're really good."

"Oh, yeah, I've heard them before. They're great. Maybe I'll . . . we'll go down there later."

I really didn't want Gio sitting there when Olivia came back, but I couldn't think of a way to get rid of him that didn't seem suspicious.

"What are you guys doing tonight?" I asked.

They looked at each other. "Maybe a movie?" Gio said.

"Sure. Do we have to eat dinner with your father first?"

Gio shook his head. "Nope. He's otherwise engaged. As usual."

"Not that I *mind*," Diana said.

"Of course you mind. Anyone would mind. *I* mind," Gio said.

And that was what they were talking about when Olivia Frost returned. She didn't immediately recognize Gio from the class, but he recognized her.

I introduced Diana, reminded Olivia how she knew Gio, and then let them all just stare at each other for a minute trying to figure out the connections. Gio seemed to think he'd get an explanation by boring a hole through my brain with his eyes.

Diana was one of those very sensitive types who always pick up on any tension between others, and I guess she thought she'd defuse whatever was going on by chattering to Olivia.

"Here I am standing with three soon-to-be novelists. I'm so impressed that you're really doing it. I write too, but I could never sustain anything as long as a novel. I don't see how anybody can. I mean, when you start out, how do you know you'll ever reach the end of it? It's terrifying."

Olivia bestowed a smile on Diana. "Writing a novel is like driving a car at night. You can only see as far as your headlights, but you can make the whole trip that way."

"Oh, I love that!" Diana said. "Do you mind if I write that down?" She started plowing through her bag looking for something to write on.

Even Gio nodded. "Yeah, that makes sense. I like that idea."

I liked it too. I liked almost everything about Olivia Frost.

Diana and Gio left soon after that, and Olivia slid in close to me on the bench. She took out her new grape earrings and slipped them into her ears, then shook her head so they sparkled. I was appreciating the way they looked with her hair when suddenly she took something else out of her purse and pressed it into my hand.

"Don't say anything," Olivia demanded. "I have the money, and this necklace was made for you."

The amber pendant sparkled on my palm. "But . . . but . . . you shouldn't . . . I can't . . ."

"No, I won't listen to any objections. It's yours." She smiled wholeheartedly. "I would accept a hug, though, if you felt inclined to give me one."

After Olivia slipped the necklace over my head, I gave her an awkward hug, fearing that full body contact might make me melt. Besides, what was the protocol for hugging your teacher right out in public, anyway? I hoped Gio and Diana were no longer in our vicinity.

To make up for my anemic embrace I thanked Olivia effusively, but I had the feeling I'd disappointed her. After a minute she looked at her watch, frowned, declared she had somewhere to be, and disappeared into the crowd.

CHAPTER TEN

I FELT LIKE KICKING MYSELF. The most gorgeous, brilliant woman had just bought me lunch and followed that up with jewelry—which must mean *something*—and I was afraid to give her a decent hug! It was too confusing—was Olivia Frost really interested in *me*? What was going on here?

I started to wander through the crowd in a sleepwalking daze, headed nowhere.

"Marisol!" somebody called. "Marisol! Over here!"

Now what? I forced my eyes to focus on Lee, headed toward me with an ice cream cone dripping down over her fist like a little kid. It was a relief to see her—somebody completely unconnected to my current discombobulation or the screwups of last spring.

"Hey," I said. "You could use a napkin."

"Always the helpful waitress," she said, licking some of the drips. "Are you here alone?"

"Not really. I mean, my friend was with me, but she had to leave."

"I'm here with my sister. She's over there looking at some photographs. Do you want to meet her?"

"Sure."

When we located her, Lindsay had three black and white portraits lined up and was trying to decide between them. "Nice to meet you, Marisol. Lee told me about hanging out at the Mug with you. I'm glad she's made a friend."

Lee rolled her eyes at her sister's comment, and I knew it embarrassed her. As if being Lee's friend were a good deed for which I should be thanked.

Nobody would ever pick Lindsay as Lee's sister. They were both fairly tall, but that was about it for resemblance. Lindsay had reddish-blond hair pulled into a heavy braid that fell down her back, and she was larger than Lee, although most of the weight was in her hips and boobs. And she certainly didn't dress in that kind of uniform invisibility that Lee preferred: Lindsay had on a long, bright pink skirt and a black tank top cut low enough to elicit stares from a good portion of the males in the vicinity. She was pretty, but not in a knockout kind of way—in more of an I-know-I'm-pretty-but-let's-not-make-a-big-deal-out-of-it kind of way. No makeup, no fancy shoes, no glamour.

"Which of these do you guys like?" she asked.

"Why do you want a picture of somebody you don't even know?" Lee said. "Won't everybody ask you who it is?"

"I like the idea of having a picture of somebody I don't know—it's mysterious. Besides, it's the lighting that's really magical about these. What do you think, Marisol?"

I had to admit that the photos were dramatic. "I like how that one has the girl standing in deep shadow so you notice her outline more than her face."

"Oh, I'm glad you like that one—I think that's my

favorite too. I feel like she has a secret, don't you? I think I could look at this picture forever and wonder who she is and what's going on in her head."

"So I guess I'll have to look at it forever too," Lee said, but it seemed more like a sibling habit of kvetching rather than real annoyance.

"Only until you leave for college," Lindsay said. "Assuming you apply to college."

"Assuming I graduate from high school," Lee shot back.

They glared at each other for a minute, and then Lindsay turned to me. "Lee says you're going to Stanford next year. How come so far away?"

"My parents live here, in Cambridge. I wanted to put some distance between us. Not that we don't get along—we do. It just seemed like farther would be better. You know, to get a fresh start."

Lindsay nodded. "I guess. Although once you're away from home, you're away. It doesn't really matter how far you go. Everything changes. And when you go back, it's all different. You're still a family, but not in the same way. You're a split-up family—you can never go back to being a kid in that house again. It's a little bit sad."

I couldn't imagine that would be true for me. Surely, I would be Mama Guzman's beloved orphan child until we were both white-haired and senile. Still, if it was true for Lindsay, maybe it was true for Lee, too.

Lee turned abruptly back to the photographs, cutting off her sister's train of thought. "If you're going to buy one, buy the one Marisol likes. It could be anybody. It could be me."

Lindsay looked at the photograph again. "You're right, Lee—it does look sort of like you. I'm getting that one!" She picked it up and took it to the cashier to pay.

Lee kept her face turned away from me until the tightness in her jaw relaxed and she'd swallowed back the threatening tears. She hadn't, I thought, really made a choice to leave home; the decision had been foisted upon her by the rest of her family. But surely she'd wanted to leave Indiana. I thought of Olivia longing to get out of her midwestern hometown and come east. Maybe Lee didn't realize yet how lucky she was. She might not have chosen Cambridge, but it was a great place to be, especially with her parents half a continent away.

I was fingering my new necklace when she turned back.

"That's pretty. Did you just get it?"

"Um, yeah. My . . . friend got it for me."

Lee nodded and thought that over. "So, your friend is a . . . girlfriend?"

"Not exactly. I mean, I'm not sure. I guess she might be." Just saying that much out loud made me a little dizzy. I had no idea what I was to Olivia Frost, besides her "star" student. But I certainly wanted to be something more than that, and I wanted Lee to think I was something more too.

Lee nodded and forced a grin. "I'd like to meet her sometime." Well, that was obviously a lie, but it was the one kind of lie I could easily forgive, the kind with which you try to save yourself a little pain.

It was becoming obvious that Lee had a crush on me, and I felt like kind of a jerk for not responding to her. I knew she was lonely and just out of that passé closet; she probably didn't even know any other lesbians. Hell, I didn't know that many either, unless you counted the New York zine people. There had been a few lesbians in my prep school's gay-straight alliance, but they'd all gone off to college. Probably not a bad idea for me to ferret out some more local lesbians—if nothing else it would show Lee that I wasn't the only available choice.

That's when it occurred to me that a road trip might be in order. And I knew just the place.

"Oh, can I come along too?" Birdie begged. "I've never even been to Provincetown, which is so unfair. There's a boat you can take over from Boston on the weekends!"

I sighed. "The boat is expensive, Birdie. By the time we pay for a place to stay, and food . . . and besides, you'll want to bring Damon along, whereas I would really love to have a vacation *from* Damon, not *with* him."

"You don't even try to get to know him. You don't give him a chance, Marisol. He's a sweet potato!"

"Well, you say potato, I say brussels sprout."

Suddenly a rapturous look came over Birdie's face, and he sucked in a lungful of excitement. "You know what? My mother has these clients, these guys who own a place in P'town that her real estate office rents out for them when they aren't there. I've seen pictures of this place, and it's gorgeous, right on the bay downtown! They spend the month of August there, but they're never around in September."

"So? It must rent for a fortune if it's that good. Just because your mother pays your rent doesn't mean she'd pay for an expensive vacation house."

He shook his head madly. "No, no, they told her she could have it free sometime when they weren't there. They love my mother—they make a bundle off the rentals she sets up. You know my mother; she's such a fag hag."

"Why doesn't she go herself?"

"Too busy. Workaholic and all. And I think she's afraid if she spent any time in P'town, she'd never want to come back."

"And why would these clients let a bunch of teenagers have their place for a weekend?"

"Well, sweetheart, you never know unless you ask!"

And so the plan began to take shape. Birdie's mother called her clients, explained the situation, told them how shy and well-behaved her son and all his friends were, and the deal was brokered. Birdie printed out photos from a website of the luxurious living room, the deck over the beach, the hot tub with a view of the stars.

Before I'd even called Lee to ask her about it, Damon was shrieking gleefully in the living room. "Oh, my God! This is going to be the highlight of my year!" Which is how my quiet little road trip morphed into an all-out cavalcade of homosexual delight. Now all we had to do was come up with a weekend when all four of us could go before the weather got too cold to enjoy it.

Lee was stunned at the suggestion. "I thought you had a girlfriend?"

"It's not like that. I mean, yeah, I might be starting something up with this woman, but I'm not going to be spending every minute with her. She's older; she's busy. And besides, this would just be friends taking a weekend trip. You really have to see Provincetown, Lee. There's no place like it—it's a gay paradise. It'll make you glad you live on the East Coast."

"That's a goal to shoot for," she said. "You're not just trying to find me a girlfriend, are you?"

"No!" I said. "I mean, you never know who you'll meet there. You could meet somebody you like."

She frowned. "That's what I was afraid of."

"Come on, Lee. We'll have a good time; I promise. I have the weekend of the twenty-sixth and twenty-seventh off work, so that would be the best for me. The boys can do that one too. What do you think?"

"I don't know, Marisol."

"The water on the Cape is warmer in September than any other time of the year."

"Don't you have your writing class on Saturday mornings?"

"I'll just have to miss one," I said, wondering what I'd tell Olivia about skipping her class. "Think of it as a field trip!"

"Maybe it would be fun. And God knows I have nothing to do *any* weekend. Let me clear it with my sister."

"Great! If the boat isn't too expensive, that would be a cool way to go. Otherwise we'll have to take the bus."

"I don't mind the bus. That's how I got out here."

Now I was surprised. "You came all the way from Indiana on a bus?"

"Yup. Took two days and I switched buses five times."

"That's horrible!"

"No, it was actually fun. You meet all kinds of people. Sometimes they get on in the middle of the night, in the middle of nowhere, and disappear by dawn. Sometimes they tell you their life stories and then fall asleep on your shoulder."

"Oh, my God—do they drool on you?"

Lee laughed. "You're a snob, you know that, Marisol? You need a nice long bus trip. It'll make you glad there's more to the United States than just the East Coast."

CHAPTER ELEVEN

I'D BEEN SITTING AT MY DESK for an hour already without putting a word on the page. One problem was that my fingers kept straying from the keyboard to play with my necklace, to feel its weight and to pull it away from my shirt so I could admire it. Without the hard evidence of that amber stone I knew I would begin to doubt the facts of my unlikely afternoon with Olivia Frost.

And then, suddenly, I knew what would happen to Christina, my protagonist, the dental receptionist who was lucky in everything but love. She would meet somebody a little older, somebody she couldn't manipulate or even understand the way she did her younger friends. And this woman—yes, it had to be a woman—would be brilliant and beautiful.

Okay, it wasn't an idea whispered in my ear by some ancient muse; it was basically the story of my current life. But you used the material you had. And writing about Christina was exciting because she wasn't me—or rather, she *was* me, only funnier and luckier and much more clever. Christina could immediately come up with all the wiseass remarks I usually didn't think of until hours later. The advice Olivia had given us about dialogue was a big help—Christina could talk people's ears off. Once I got started, I didn't want to stop. I wrote almost ten pages before I made myself quit and take a shower so I could get to work on time.

The hours at the Mug dragged. I kept thinking of scenes I could be writing between Christina and her older woman friend, who I didn't have a perfect name for yet. Around two o'clock there was literally nobody in the restaurant for twenty minutes, so I sat with the phone book on my lap, making another list of names.

Vanessa
Ava
Blythe
Tess
Cecilia
Elana
Aviva
Geneva
Juliette
Grace
Nicole
Siena

I was so aggravated when the next customers came in and interrupted me that I made these two skinny college girls order pie even though they clearly only wanted coffee. If you get on the wrong side of me, I'm going to make you *eat*.

By late afternoon the place got busy, and I had to give up even thinking about writing. Lee was ensconced in her usual booth, but fortunately I was not talking to her when Doug came storming in the back door. He was wearing a sweatshirt, high-water pants, and an old, scuffed pair of sneakers—not his usual working attire. It didn't look like he'd shaved in a few days either, and the overall effect was similar to that of the homeless men who sometimes slept in Harvard Square doorways on cold nights.

He waved me back into the kitchen with Sophie and the other cook, Pete.

"Just wanted to tell everybody," he mumbled, "Gus is back home. I just settled him in at his place with a bucketful of pills to take."

"Oh, that's great," Sophie said. "He's a tough old guy."

"Yeah, well, here's the thing, Sophie. Gus and me have been talking it over. He ain't gonna last forever, you know, and once he's gone, this place will go too."

"But Doug, didn't you once say that Gus was planning to leave the place to you?" Pete asked.

"That was years back, when I was a younger man. I'm no spring chicken anymore either. Once Gus is gone, I don't want to worry about making ends meet around here. I'd have to sell the place. I've only kept it running this long because it's Gus's place and he loves it."

"Whoever buys it would keep it open, wouldn't they?" I asked.

Doug shook his head. "Not as a rundown old coffee shop. This is valuable real estate."

"What? You mean they'd tear down the Mug and put up a . . . a Starbucks or something?" Even as I said it, I felt guilty.

Who was I to complain about Starbucks?

"I don't know what would go in, but something that would make more money than the Mug, I know that. Anyway, I'm telling you this because I think you should all be aware of it. If a better opportunity comes along for you, you shouldn't hesitate to take it. You've been a loyal bunch, but I know you all got bills to pay."

Guilt and more guilt. Not everyone's mother was slipping them money to pay the rent.

"I'll stick around," Pete said. "I can always get something if we close up."

Sophie bit her lip. "Doug, I have to confess, when you said Gus was in the hospital again, I went through the want ads. I figured it would come to this eventually, and I can't afford to retire completely just yet. I have an interview tomorrow afternoon for a part-time job at a bakery up in Arlington. Near my daughter's house."

"Well, I hope you get the job, Sophie. If you want it, you take it. I can't make you any promises here anymore," Doug said sadly. "I hope Gus hangs on awhile longer, but you never know from one day to the next."

Doug turned his face away and squinted his eyes. I wondered if he was just feeling the impending loss of an old, close friend, or if their relationship was more complicated than that. Or maybe all relationships were more complicated than they seemed on the surface.

Even though I'd only wandered into the Mug two or three times before I started working there, the demise of the place seemed to herald something larger, like perhaps the collapse of western civilization. How many unique places were left in Harvard Square? Not more than a handful, and now the place where T. S. Eliot might just possibly have sipped his tea was going under too. It was depressing.

Lee waited for my shift to finish at six; we sat in the pit by the T stop for a while, and I told her what Doug had said.

"I hope they don't close the Mug," she said. "I was just starting to feel like it was my place. I mean, someplace friendly to go where I recognized a few people."

I nodded. "I'm pretty attached to my paycheck, too. Where am I gonna work if the Mug closes?"

"Where am I gonna hang out?"

We stared glumly at our shoes for a few minutes.

"I told my mother about you last night on the phone," I said, finally, just to fill the empty space that was bearing down on our shoulders.

"You did?"

I nodded. "Yeah. She got all excited about meeting you. You'll have to go over there with me one of these days."

"She wants to meet me?" Lee's voice was kind of squeaky.

"Maybe I didn't tell you—she's the standard-bearer for the local PFLAG chapter. The minute I came out to her, she became an expert on the subject of homosexuality and how it affects teenagers. I make fun of her, but really, she's great. I can't imagine not having her support. Anyway, when I told her about you having to leave Indiana because your parents *weren't* supportive, she wanted to know what she could do about it. She wanted to send your parents brochures, call them up, get to be their new best friend. Can you imagine?"

I shook my head. "She's too much sometimes."

Lee banged her heel against the wall. "My parents aren't *that* bad. I mean, they didn't kick me out or anything. They just couldn't handle it very well."

"I know. That's what I told her, but she gets very excited about this stuff."

"So, that's why she wants to meet me? To help me?"

"Or maybe to adopt you; I'm not sure." I meant it as a joke, but Lee frowned, and we fell silent again.

Finally she said, "When are you working tomorrow?"

"I'm not. Day off. Why?"

She shrugged. "I don't know. I was thinking of cutting my afternoon classes. Maybe we could hang out."

"Really? You're skipping school?" I said, as though it were a foreign concept to me. What I was really thinking was, *Damn, I want to write tomorrow.*

"I only have trig and English after lunch."

"Yeah, like *those* aren't important. You better not."

Lee turned and glared at me. "Marisol, I'll cut school if I want to. You aren't my mother, you know!"

"You're the one who was telling your sister you might not even graduate. You can't afford to skip—"

"I just said that to make her crazy. I'm doing fine. And by the way, you aren't my guardian angel, either, so stop acting like it."

My mouth fell open. "What are you talking about?"

"I'm talking about you and your mother discussing my poor orphanhood and what can be done to help me. I'm seventeen, Marisol. I don't need a babysitter. If that's what you want to be, I suggest you get yourself a nanny job." She jumped off the wall and started to walk away. "And I don't need a pimp, either. I can find my own girlfriends!"

I got down and ran after her. "Hey, what's the problem here? Just because I try to help you a little bit—"

"I don't need your help!" she yelled. People at a sidewalk café stared at us, but we kept on marching.

"Of course you do. You don't even know anybody else!"

She stopped walking and glared at me. "Do you have to keep reminding me of how *pathetic* I am? Believe me, I understand that without you pointing it out to me!"

Where was this coming from? "Lee, I don't think you're pathetic at all. I don't know where you got that idea." I tried to grab for her arm, but she pulled away from me.

"I have to go home, Marisol."

"Do you want me to walk with you?"

"No, I don't! God, you think I can't even walk six blocks by myself! Leave me alone!" She was starting to cry by then, so I backed away. I was stumped by the source of all that anger, but maybe it had more to do with her lousy relationship with her parents than it did with me. Maybe she just needed to let off some steam.

In fact, I couldn't have cared less whether she went to school the next day or not. But I had my own idea of how I wanted to spend the afternoon, and it would only have upset her more if she knew. My laptop and I were going to get going on chapter two, and we were planning to do it, God help us, at Starbucks.

Chapter Twelve

IT WAS A BAD SIGN that I could smell our third-floor apartment the minute I walked through the downstairs door. And it wasn't just the seldom-cleaned cat box either—this was some kind of dog disaster.

I opened the apartment door to find Birdie and Damon glaring at each other while Noodles cowered behind the couch. Birdie's salvaged red rug was now literally crappy, dribbled from edge to edge with soupy puppy poop. The stench was overwhelming.

"God, what happened?" I said, putting my hand over my nose and mouth to try to filter the incoming air.

"I'll tell you what happened," Birdie said. "Even though I've told Damon a hundred times not to leave his stupid candy bars lying out on the table where Noodles can get them, he did it anyway. And guess what?"

"How could she jump that high? You should put her in a circus," Damon said. "Besides, if you'd taken her for a walk when you said you were going to, this mess would be on the sidewalk and not in the living room."

"Great, then the neighbors could enjoy it too," I said. "I

should rub both your noses in it." But my presence was barely noticed.

"You made my dog sick, Damon, and my rug is ruined. Your fault—not mine!" Birdie was so steamed, I figured there was something more behind this than dog poop.

Damon pointed to the matted shag under his feet with revulsion. "This filthy thing? You're upset about *this*? Believe me, it was disgusting long before Noodles crapped on it. Good riddance to it!" Had to agree with Damon on that one—sometimes the big lug made sense. I looked to Birdie for the next volley. Aside from the odor this event was somewhat entertaining.

Birdie slammed it over the net. "Who eats candy bars, anyway? I haven't had a candy bar since I was ten years old! Which could be why I don't have a million zits on my face like *some* people!" *Ouch.*

Damon's face (with, actually, no more than one small zit that I could see) reddened. "It's none of your business what I eat. Besides," he said sheepishly, "I only eat the little ones." Oops. Never let your opponent see weakness.

"Yeah, twenty little ones at a time!" Birdie shot back. Game, set, match.

For a minute I thought Damon might smack Birdie, but instead he picked Noodles's leash off the back of the door and called her over. "I'll take the poor animal—about whom you care so *deeply*—for a walk. And I'll take her to the vet clinic to make sure she's okay, too, because I do actually care about her welfare."

That was one good thing about Damon—he was better about walking Noodles than Birdie and me combined. He slammed the door behind him, and I looked to Birdie for a further explanation.

"He never listens to me," Birdie said.

"About the candy bars?"

"About anything!" He sighed. "Help me roll this up and take it down to the Dumpster."

"Gladly."

"What? You don't like it either?"

"No, I don't! And I wish you'd stop pretending this is all about rugs and candy bars. What's going on?"

We moved the couch back and started rolling the rug before he answered me. "I don't know exactly. I guess it's harder than I thought to live with somebody you like."

The smell was making me dizzy. I rolled faster, which only made the tube uneven. "You know, you jumped into this pretty quickly, Birdie. You barely knew Damon when you invited him to live here." Give me a medal for not saying, *I told you so.*

I got the length of clothesline I used for drying underwear in my bedroom when I didn't feel like trekking to the Laundromat, and we tied it around the carpet, then hoisted the miserable thing to our shoulders. A long bath would be necessary after this job.

Birdie sighed as we started down the stairs. "He just seemed so perfect at first."

Perfect? On what planet?

"Nobody's perfect," I said, "but if it's not working out, you should ask him to leave. He can probably still get a dorm room." It's hard to cross your fingers while carrying a large rug.

We maneuvered the thing through the downstairs doorway and around the corner to the trash bins.

"I can't ask him to leave," Birdie said.

"Sure you can. You just say, 'Please leave.' I'd even be willing to say it for you, if necessary."

"No, you don't understand, Marisol. I love Damon!"

We gave a hearty heave, and the stinky shag was history. Unfortunately, Damon was not.

"You *love* him? You were just yelling at him about having zits!"

He sighed. "I know. I'm a terrible person. Being in love makes me emotionally unstable."

"Don't blame love," I muttered as we trudged back upstairs.

"I shouldn't have said that stuff about the candy bars, either. He doesn't really eat that many at a time. But he leaves them out on the table after I told him not to! He doesn't listen to me! What am I going to do?" he whined.

Crap. I was obviously going to have to make my peace with Damon if Birdie was going to go all heartbreaky on me.

"Well, maybe if you *asked* him not to leave the candy bars out instead of *telling* him. You're not the president of the apartment, you know."

"God, I'm horribly difficult to live with, aren't I? I said I'd walk Noodles hours ago, but I wanted to listen to my new CD first, and then I got a couple of phone calls, and . . . Damon probably hates me now. And he's so sweet, don't you think, Marisol?"

"Sweet as tooth decay," I said. And, obviously, just as hard to get rid of.

"You have a couple of messages on the machine," Birdie said when we got back to the apartment. He went for the pine-scented cleaner while I punched play. I figured one of them would be from Lee, who probably felt remorseful about yelling at me by the time she walked home. But no, nothing from Lee.

"Uh, hi. This is Gio. I hope it's okay that I called. I'm kind of having a problem doing the writing assignment this week. You know, about the setting. It's hard to describe some-place you haven't actually been. But I'm afraid this means I can only write about Boston or Darlington, Massachusetts. Anyway, I thought you might have some thoughts about it. Call me if you have time."

Great! Gio wanted to talk about writing, the topic which had bonded us to begin with. I figured I'd call him back right away, until I heard message number two, delivered in a low, slow voice.

"Hello, Marisol. This is Olivia. I've been thinking about you. How about meeting me for breakfast Saturday morning before class starts? I have an appointment in the afternoon, so I won't be able to have lunch, and I want to see you. Call me."

Birdie, of course, was eavesdropping. "I just have two questions," he said. "First of all, you're seeing *Gio* again? Are you insane? Do you not remember what happened last time? And secondly, who the hell is this Olivia, and is she as hot as she sounds?"

"Yes to all of the above," I said, then took the cordless phone into my room and closed the door.

I called Olivia first because just hearing her voice made my stomach flip, and I wasn't sure I could speak to anybody else until I'd made contact with her. But she wasn't home, so I had to leave a message in my own unique tongue: Angstlish.

"Hey! Hi, Olivia. This is Marisol. I got your message, so I'm calling back, but you aren't there. Anyway, thanks again for the beautiful necklace, which I've been wearing every day. Well, most days, anyway. So, yes, I would love to meet you for breakfast on Saturday before class. Should we meet at the Center or somewhere else? The Center is fine, or wherever you want. And I'm really looking forward to class, too—God, can you hear that loud sucking noise? I'm going to shut the hell up now because I sound like a fricking moron."

By the time I put the phone down, my armpits were swampy and my knees had come unglued. What the hell? I never acted this dorky! Just because Olivia was older and brilliant and my teacher and looked like she should be cast in a Pedro Almodóvar movie . . . I had to rest for ten minutes or so until I had the strength to call Gio.

Thank God that was easy. He launched right into his problem with the assignment.

"Maybe the problem is that I'm not actually writing a novel," he said, sighing. "I'm just doing the assignments to stir up ideas for a story or something. But I really don't want to write about Darlington, Massachusetts. I'm there too many hours during my actual life; I don't want to spend my imaginary time there too."

"There must be some other places you know well enough to use. Some place you've visited that you remember."

"My parents took one vacation before they got divorced, and it was a total disaster. We went to a dude ranch in

Wyoming, and my mother fell off a horse the first day and broke her arm. We stayed all week, though, so Dad could get in all the ridin' and ropin' he'd paid for. Mom sat on the porch trying to knit one-handed. I stayed inside the cabin and read comic books."

"Well, that's not too promising, since it sounds like you didn't actually *see* much of Wyoming."

"Nope."

"It's a good story, though. You ought to write it up anyway. Not for class, just for your zine."

"Yeah, maybe I will. But I still need a place to describe for the exercise. What are you writing about?"

"Cambridge. The novel will be set there and in Boston."

"That's convenient."

"You could use Boston too, couldn't you? The Back Bay, where your dad lives. All those old brownstones with the tidy little yards—there are some mighty metaphors hiding in that landscape."

"Wait! I've got it! I know what I can write about!" Gio all but screamed.

"And it is . . ."

"Provincetown! It'll be easy—there's no place like it, right? All the funny little ancient houses crowded together on the main street, the smell of the bay and the fishing boats, the bars, the crazy crowds. That's it!"

Of course I remembered it all too. I'd been fascinated to walk into that gorgeous gay mecca, but I hadn't been able to fully enjoy it because of the achy knot in my chest. I'd been determined to make it clear to Gio that weekend that we were never going to be more than just friends, even if it hurt him so much that he couldn't actually *be* my friend anymore. It had been a memorable trip, but not an easy one.

"I should've thought of it sooner," he continued. "Did I tell you I'm going down there the Saturday after this one to see Diana for the weekend? She lives in Truro, but we'll go into Provincetown to go dancing and hang out."

That was the weekend I'd planned to go down to the Cape with Lee, Birdie, and Damon. Now Gio was going to be there too? What lousy timing. I should have just told him right then that I was going too, but I thought about it a few seconds too long and the obvious moment to say something passed. Maybe he didn't need to know. It was a small town, but always crowded—what were the chances we'd bump into him? And if he knew I was going to be there, he'd feel like we should all meet up or something, and that would be too awkward. Birdie would make some poisonous remark, and ugh, I could just see the entire weekend going to hell in a handbasket for all of us.

"Are you taking the boat or the bus?" I asked.

"Bus, I guess."

"Well, have a great time!" I said, wondering just how expensive boat tickets could be and who was going to spring for the four we needed.

CHAPTER THIRTEEN

SINCE I DIDN'T HAVE TO WORK the next day, I slept later than usual and was just getting out of the shower when the doorbell rang. Birdie and Damon, who seemed to have patched up their candy bar conflict, had already left for class, so I wrapped a towel around myself and called downstairs on the intercom to see who it was.

"It's me, Lee."

"Oh, good," I said. "I'll buzz you in."

I had intended to call her after my shower, but here she was, the little truant. She must have cooled off since the afternoon before. I was glad to be able to sort out the problem now so I'd still have most of the day free to write.

I unlatched the apartment door, tucked the towel in a little tighter around my chest, and waited for her to trudge up the stairs. She looked up at me as she climbed, her face blank and not entirely friendly. She took in my state of undress and looked back down at the stair treads.

"I guess you don't get up as early as I do," she said. "I walked around for an hour or so."

"I just slept in a little this morning." I closed the door behind her.

"I had to leave the house when my sister did so she'd think I went to school. I figured it was easier to just skip the whole day."

"Right." I wasn't falling into that trap again—skip school if you want to, no skin off my nose. We stood there looking and not looking at each other for an uncomfortable minute.

Finally I said, "Have you had breakfast yet?" hoping that didn't sound too maternal.

She shook her head. "I don't usually eat breakfast."

I bit my tongue to staunch my usual lecture on the health benefits of having a good meal in the morning. "Let me go get dressed and I'll scramble us some eggs. You can start a pot of coffee if you want. Coffee and filters are in the cupboard over the coffeemaker." I motioned her toward the kitchen.

"I haven't . . . I guess I don't know how to make coffee." She sounded so defeated, as though failure as a barista were the last straw. Of course, *I* thought being able to brew a decent cup of coffee was a necessary life skill, but it wasn't on the final exam or anything.

"It's easy," I said. "Fill the pot to the eight-cups mark, which will really only make enough for about four decent-sized mugs, and pour it into the water receptacle. There's a scoop in the coffee—put four healthy scoops into the filter you've put into the filter basket. Close it up, turn it on, wait three minutes: coffee."

She nodded. "I'll try."

I headed into my bedroom to figure out what to wear to accidentally run into Olivia later in the day, assuming she showed up at Starbucks again. I didn't want to look like I'd dressed for a date, but I didn't want to look too cruddy either—and the choices were limited.

Lee, I noticed, was in her usual cloak of invisibility: jeans and white T-shirt with a jean jacket thrown over the top against the morning chill. Staring at myself in the mirror, I was grateful to have spent very little of my lifetime thus far worrying about clothes—it was much too frustrating. I put on my black work pants; they were not the cleanest, but I could dab at the spots of dried tuna salad and spilled coffee to make them a little more respectable. I had a brick-red T-shirt that looked good under my black and white flannel shirt—the combination seemed like an outfit that didn't absolutely scream, *I dressed especially for you,* but neither did it say, *I don't give a shit what I look like.*

Finally, I put the amber pendant on and took it off again half a dozen times, then left it on my dresser top so that Lee wouldn't feel stung by its appearance.

When I walked into the kitchen, Lee was sitting at the table with a mug of heavily milked coffee in front of her into which she was ladling spoonfuls of sugar. I couldn't help flashing back to last spring, when I'd forced Gio to drink coffee and he too sugared and milked it into something more closely resembling coffee ice cream.

"God, I just remembered—you drink tea, not coffee. I'm such a bully," I said.

"It's okay," Lee said. "It's pretty good this way."

No lecture from me on how the only way to drink coffee is black. I poured myself a dark cup. "Not bad for your first attempt," I told her, though it was definitely weaker than I'd have made it myself.

I checked the fridge and found three eggs and one lone marble bagel. "Do you want scrambled eggs? Or I could make you an over easy, whichever."

"Scrambled is fine," Lee said.

"One bagel left—you want to split it?"

"Sure." She squirmed in her chair, and I had the feeling she was trying to say something and I wasn't giving her the opportunity. So I shut up and started the scrambling process, sliced the bagel, got two plates out of the cupboard, and pretended she wasn't even there. Finally she assembled the words in her mouth.

"I'm sorry about yesterday," she said.

"Don't worry about it. I'm sure I was being a brat again."

She waved her hand as if to shush me. "No, you weren't. I just . . . I just get so homesick sometimes, I can't stand it. It feels like I've lost my whole world and it's my own fault. I've been transplanted into this foreign place, and nothing will ever be the same. My feelings seep out and discolor everything, like bruises. Even my food tastes sour."

Wow. I was suddenly kind of impressed with Lee. I guess it was the first time I thought of her as someone other than just a needy kid, a lost soul who I could help. This was obviously someone who wrestled with her emotions and scrutinized the consequences of her actions the same way I did.

"I feel like you don't even know the real Lee O'Brien," she continued. "The person I was back in Indiana. I'm different here. I'm alone, I'm lonely, and that makes me feel awful and act terrible. I was more fun back at home! People liked me!"

"I'm sure people liked you in Indiana," I told her. "You're fun *here*. I don't think you're the pathetic person you think you are."

But she didn't agree. "You don't know. I'm different now. I'm gray, I'm glum, I'm . . . invisible."

That shook me a little, since "invisible" was indeed how I often thought of Lee, but I certainly wouldn't tell her that. "Look, you've gone through a lot of changes in the last month or so. You came out to your family and friends. You moved halfway across the country, started a new school. Of course you feel different, but inside you're still the same person you've always been. I think you're too impatient. Give yourself time to adjust."

She sighed. "Well, I don't have much choice, do I?"

I sprinkled the eggs with pepper, oregano, and Parmesan cheese. "Wait'll you taste my eggs," I said. "That'll cheer you up."

"You do cheer me up," she said. "You're the only one who does."

Oh, dear. Were we entering dangerous territory again?

"Next time you see Birdie, ask him how cheerful I am to live with. I think he'll give you a second opinion." I plopped the bagel slice and half the eggs on a plate and set it in front of her. "Now, eat up," I demanded, impersonating a crotchety cowpoke.

I worked hard to get the conversation on a lighter plane. By the time we finished eating we'd discussed the best and worst meals our mothers had ever cooked; the half dozen hamsters Lee had had growing up, all of which lived exactly one year; swimming lessons at age nine (hers); dancing lessons at age five (mine); and my history with Birdie, up to and including the pooped-on red shag rug. Lee perked up, and I began to see the funny, friendly person whose disappearance she'd been worried about.

"I think I'm going to like Birdie," she said. "I used to be a Dumpster diver myself, you know."

"Really? What was your best find?" I asked.

"Well, let's see, I found a hula girl lamp one time, but it didn't work anymore, so I used it to hold my baseball caps. And I found an excellent comic book collection, which I'm sure someone's mother threw out when they weren't looking. I made a nice little wad of cash selling those on eBay."

"Wow, you got better stuff than Birdie does!"

"Yeah, until the time I brought home this nice fleecy blanket and put it on my bed without washing it first—"

"Oh, this is going to have a bad ending, isn't it?"

"Oh, yeah. Apparently the blanket was infested with some kind of horrible bedbug creatures—"

"No!"

"I got bitten to pieces, and we ended up having to throw out my mattress and wash every sheet and curtain and piece of clothing in the room. Actually, my mother ended up calling an exterminator."

"She must have freaked out."

"Oh, my God. I was the one covered with bug bites, but she was scratching at herself for weeks. That was my last Dumpster dive."

"Very sad."

"Tragic," she said, laughing. It was so nice to see her leaning back in her chair, looking relaxed and happy. I knew I could have spent the rest of the day with Lee and enjoyed myself. I might have suggested we go to the Brattle Theatre for a matinee of one of those Tennessee Williams movies she loved. It wouldn't have been a sacrifice at all. Except I kept thinking that Olivia could already be sitting at a table in Starbucks, and I wasn't there with her.

I glanced at the clock; it was almost noon. Jeez, we'd been sitting here for hours already! I stacked the plates one on the other and stood to put them in the sink.

"You didn't want more coffee, did you?" I asked Lee.

"No, I've had plenty. Let me wash the dishes for you," she said.

I waved her off as I threw the napkins in the trash and flicked off the coffeepot. "No need. I'll do them later, when I get back."

"You have plans for the day?" she asked.

"Yeah, well, I have that writing course, you know? And I need to work on my assignment for this week's class."

"Right! I hope I didn't hold you up."

"No, you didn't. It was fun. But, you know, I should get started on it."

"Okay. Well, thanks for breakfast," she said, her mood much improved from when she entered the apartment.

"Any time you're in the neighborhood," I said, following her from the kitchen to the front door.

"I might take you up on that," she said. Then, after a

slight hesitation, she leaned forward and gave me a quick hug. The long bones of her arms held me as lightly as if they were shadows, and my face rested briefly against her lemony-soap-smelling neck.

"See you soon!" she called as she flew down the stairs.

I made her no promises, even though the hug, invisible as it was, had left a surprising imprint.

CHAPTER FOURTEEN

OLIVIA WAS THERE. At one of the really small tables near the door. Barely room for one laptop—certainly not two.

She looked up and smiled the minute I walked in, as though she'd been expecting me. "Look who's here," she said.

As I got near the table, she closed her laptop, and I couldn't help feeling a tiny bit insulted. Like she thought I was going to read over her shoulder or steal her work or something. Not that I wasn't awfully curious about what was on her hard drive. And I had to admit, it bugged the hell out of me when Birdie came into my room and stood there looking at my screen over my shoulder.

"I got so much work done here last time, I thought I'd try it again," I said.

She nodded. "You mean you got work done until I sat down next to you."

"No! Well, I mean . . ."

"It's hard for two writers to work in the same space," Olivia said, smiling. "As soon as one types something, the other one panics. 'She's writing and I'm not!'" She pointed to a small empty table across the room. "Sit over there. We'll work for an hour or two and then you can join me, okay?"

"Good idea," I said, wondering how I was going to keep my eyes on the monitor and not her soft blue sweater. But, I retreated to my table, got a large coffee, and settled in to work. It actually was much easier to work with Olivia too far away to touch or speak to. In no time the buzz of the place surrounded me, and I went into my cocoon, just me and my Mac.

The scene I wanted to write for class was the one in which Christina meets Natalie—the name I'd decided on—for the first time in a used-book store in Harvard Square. I knew the setting would play a very important part in it. I started slowly, but I seemed to know where it was going.

Christina had sought out the used-book store in Harvard Square in hopes of finding a book of short stories she could read during her breaks and lunch hour at Dr. Hester's office. She had always enjoyed short stories because of the way the best ones surprised you at the end and made you rethink everything you'd just read. They were like perfect worlds without a word out of place—everything worked together. Christina's own life was not such an orderly world, which might have been why she craved them in her reading.

The bookstore was housed in what was supposed to be one of the oldest buildings in Harvard Square. It was not on the main thoroughfare, Massachusetts Avenue, but on a side street, where it was overshadowed by the stately architecture of Harvard University. Although the building was red brick, like the Harvard edifices across the street, it lay outside the protective gates of the college itself.

As Christina entered the front door, she saw a large sign in the window announcing THIS BUILDING SOON TO BE AN OFF-PRICE MEGASTORE. She sighed regretfully. Why did things have to change? She hated change, and she almost wished she hadn't even discovered the place if it was already on its way to demolition. There could be no future for her here.

Steuben's Used Books was located in the basement of the building. There was an elevator she could have taken, but Christina put her hand on the beautifully carved newel and climbed down the wooden staircase. The treads were scuffed and scarred by the thousands of shoes that had gone before hers, searching for a Shakespeare play or a book of poetry. What would happen to all the old books once Steuben's was closed?

Christina walked the narrow, musty-smelling aisles until she found the section for short stories. There were so many to choose from, but she selected a book by Grace Paley, someone she'd always meant to read, and one by Flannery O'Connor, who she already knew she liked, and took them up to the cashier, who sat on a high stool in back of an old cash register.

"Find what you wanted?" the cashier asked. When Christina looked up at the woman's face, she was amazed at how beautiful she was. This was not the sort of woman you expected to find in a basement full of old books. Her hair was dark and shiny and swept around her shoulders as if a wind had blown in through the leaky casements for just that purpose.

At first Christina could hardly speak, but finally she forced herself to say, "Yes, thank you. I'm sorry to hear the store is closing. It must be so upsetting."

The woman shrugged. "A little, but things change."

"What will happen to all the books?"

"I'll put them into storage and sell them online," she said. "Most people want to shop that way now, anyway."

Christina made a face. "They do? You can't make a surprise discovery online! You can't see if someone has written notes on the pages! You can't find the book you wanted fallen on the floor between the bookcases! Where's the joy?"

The cashier smiled at Christina. "That's true, but most people don't want to spend time on the possibility of finding joy. They're too busy for joy. My name is Natalie, by the way. It's nice to meet you."

"I'm Christina." They shook hands.

"Oh," Natalie said. "You've chosen two of my favorite books."

"I have?"

Natalie slipped the books into a small bag. "No charge," she said. "Maybe when you're through reading them, we can talk about how much we liked them."

"What if I don't like them?" Christina said, daring to be flirtatious.

"Oh, you will," Natalie said. "I can tell already."

Christina took the bag and laughed. Through the high window behind Natalie she could see an enormous maple tree bending in the wind, its skirt of yellow leaves brushing the ground, then lifting into the air. *Surely*, she thought, *the builders won't have to cut that down too.* But maybe they would. As Natalie said, things changed—that seemed to be the only certainty in life.

The words had begun slowly and then flooded out of me. That was the only way to put it. The story was beginning to sound almost mystical, the two women kind of old-fashioned. I wasn't sure if that was what I wanted for them or not, but it interested me, and I couldn't see a reason not to follow the idea at least a little further.

I loved who Christina was becoming, a person who saw omens in a bending tree, and Natalie wasn't turning out to be as much like Olivia as I'd thought she would. The character had immediately begun to go in her own direction, pulling me along behind. It was the most exciting piece of writing I'd ever done, because it seemed to me it was something new—new for me, at least—and I had no idea where it would take me.

It was almost two hours before I came up for air. I jumped out of my chair and went over to Olivia's table, being careful to stand behind her screen so she wouldn't think I was trying to see her work.

"You finished for the day?" Olivia asked, looking up.

"I just had the most amazing writing experience! I was like, in the *zone* or something. I did the assignment, and I think it's the second chapter of my novel, too!"

"That's great," Olivia said, clicking off her laptop and closing it. "I've been making a few breakthroughs myself. We must be good for each other. Sit down."

"Are you sure you're through? I don't want to interrupt you if you aren't ready to stop working. I could wait over there—"

"Don't be silly. I'm eager to hear what you have to say about your work."

So I told her everything—well, not the part about how one of my characters was partly based on her, but everything else. About how the writing had flowed and how the characters had seemed to grow as I wrote them.

"I'm so happy for you," Olivia said, reaching across to

squeeze my hand. "It's wonderful when the writing comes easily. But don't take it for granted; for every day it's easy there are ten when it's hard."

"Do you want to hear it? I could read it to you!" If Noodles could talk, he would have sounded like me; I was practically panting.

Olivia's face closed up, and I knew I'd made a mistake.

"I'm sorry," I said. "I guess your students accost you all the time, begging you to listen to their work right this minute. I'll wait until class. It's no problem."

"It's not that, Marisol. I'm sure I'll love what you've written. It's just that I'm still in the heads of my own characters at the moment, and it's hard for me to leap from one story to another. I don't think I could give you my best attention right now. I'll be ready to hear it tomorrow."

"Sure, that's fine. But I'd be happy to listen to some of your book, if you wanted to read a little bit to me." In fact I would have been happy to listen to Olivia read the entire novel, right there, just to me. But she shook her head emphatically.

"Sorry, nobody gets a preview. If I read it out loud, or even let you read it to yourself, somehow the air goes out of it. I have to keep it to myself, my big secret, until the whole thing is finished. It keeps my energy in the book instead of worrying about what people think of it."

I was disappointed, but I understood. I just wished I were special enough to be the one person she'd let see it early.

"Do you have a title? Can you tell me that much?" I don't give up easily.

Olivia laughed. "Well, I do have a title. Must you know what it is?"

"I must."

She cleared her throat dramatically. "It is: *Lillian, Who Says She Loves You.*"

I repeated it out loud. "That's a great title," I said. "It's so mysterious. Who's Lillian?"

"No more clues! That's all you get for now." She started gathering up her possessions, and I felt a little desperate. Was she going to leave?

I looked at my watch. "Wow, it's late. I didn't even have lunch. Do you want to go somewhere, or . . . ?" God, I couldn't really ask her out, could I?

"Too late for lunch," she said. "How about dinner? As it turns out, I'm not going to be able to meet you for breakfast tomorrow—there's a Harvard faculty thing I can't skip—so let me take you someplace nice tonight. We can go home and change first. You can put on your pendant."

My hand went automatically to my neck. "Oh, I almost put it on this morning—I usually wear it—but . . . I didn't." Should I be apologizing for that?

Olivia herded me toward the door. "Well, let's go get it! My car is just down the block. The white Miata."

Olivia already looked great—what she really meant was that I should go home and change. When we walked into the apartment, Birdie and Damon were ensconced on the couch watching reruns of *The Gilmore Girls*, and I suddenly saw my living accommodations through Olivia's eyes. And they were appalling. The few measly pieces of furniture we'd gotten from Birdie's parents were cat-clawed to pieces, and the apartment was primarily accessorized by extension cords, which connected two televisions, a computer, a printer, and several lamps to the one wall socket in the room. There were hairballs and dust bunnies big enough to be live animals.

Speaking of which, Noodles scratched at Olivia's leg and Peaches attempted to leap into her unwilling arms.

"Oh, dear," she said. "I'm allergic to animals." She looked warily around the room as if the whole place was giving her hives.

Birdie jumped up. "I'll lock them in my room," he said. "Are you Olivia? You look just the way Marisol described you!"

When had I described her to Birdie? I might have said something about her hair, but . . .

I made introductions while Birdie scooted the animals out of the room.

"I guess you don't need real animals when you've got a teacher's pet," Birdie said, sweetly.

"Marisol is more than teacher's pet," Olivia said, smiling at me. "She's teacher's teacher. My best students always are."

I knew I was blushing and hoped Birdie wouldn't call attention to it. "I'm sorry the place is such a sty. I wasn't planning on having guests over," I said.

"I think it's charming," she said.

"It *is*," Birdie said as he cleared food trash off the cardboard-box coffee table. "A charming sty." At least Birdie was making a little effort; Damon just sat there staring at Olivia with a goofy smile on his face.

Olivia turned to me. "You *should* live like this when you're young and still searching for your inspirations. You aren't caught up in superficialities yet. I envy you. You aren't waiting for inspiration. You're going after it with a club."

I was? Somehow, living in a small dirty apartment with two television addicts, one of whom was mute, hadn't seemed all that inspirational to me. But if Olivia wanted to praise me, who was I to stop her? I excused myself to change clothes, wondering what on earth Birdie might say while I was gone. There was no time to waste.

The pants would have to do. In the back of my closet I found a long-sleeved black boat-neck jersey that tended to slip slyly off my shoulders—it was also long enough to cover up the tuna fish stain on my pants, so it would do nicely. There was no snazzy jacket to put over it; I'd just have to be cold if the temperature dropped. I put some mousse on my fingertips and picked at my hair until it stood out in little points—a look not everybody can get away with, but I can. Finally, I hung the amber pendant around my neck. I wasn't going to look any better than that. At least my shirt didn't have any-thing written on the back of it, like POWER TO THE PUSSY.

As I came back into the living room, Birdie was saying, "Marisol hasn't had a real girlfriend yet. There was this Kelly person who she went with for about two seconds. But Kelly traded her in for a guy, and Marisol was so—"

"Excuse me!" I interrupted him. "I can tell my own war stories, thank you."

"I was just making conversation."

"Well, make it about yourself next time."

Olivia followed me to the door, and just as we were exiting, she leaned over and stage-whispered, "You look lovely. There's fire in your eyes that matches the amber."

Bless her, she knew Birdie would be listening.

Zócalo was packed, but it only took Olivia a few minutes to get us a table. I wasn't sure if she actually knew the manager or if she could flirt that effortlessly with a complete stranger. Who cared? This incredible woman, whom everyone in the place was staring at, was here with me.

I have to admit, I was starting to wonder why. Not that I don't have a high opinion of myself—I obviously do. But Olivia was in a class by herself; she could be with anyone she wanted, and yet here she was with me. Maybe everybody felt this way when they were falling in love—I didn't know—but I kept thinking: How did this happen? I am the luckiest person in the world.

Olivia ordered herself a margarita while I settled for a ginger ale, but when she switched the glasses around on the table, no one noticed. We finished one margarita and she ordered two more while the soda remained barely touched. I didn't usually drink alcohol, since circumventing the drinking age seemed like too much effort to put in to getting a little beer buzz, but margaritas were worth the trouble. Halfway through the second one my brain was squishy and my tongue was loose.

"You know, the coffee shop where I work might have to close down soon," I said. "The Mug. They'll probably tear it down and put in a stupid food court. 'Food court.' Who ever came up with a dumb name like that, anyway? Like a tennis court with pizza slices. Or a basketball court with chicken wings. Or like the court of King George the something or other with . . . with cinnamon buns." I seemed to have no idea what my mouth was saying.

"Maybe you can get a job at the food court," Olivia suggested.

"How could I work at the food court? Warmed-over egg rolls! Bad sushi! Besides, it's practically immoral to close the Mug! T. S. Eliot ate there!"

Olivia smiled. "So they say. Personally, I always thought the place looked a little too greasy for Mr. Eliot's taste."

"You think he'd have preferred Starbucks?" I said, a little bit accusingly. "I don't think so!"

She laughed. "My little populist."

Her little populist? I was *hers* now? I grinned, and the fight went right out of me. The waiter brought our enchilada plates, and I dug in happily.

Olivia took tiny, patient bites of her meal, which I noticed only after I'd stuffed several huge forkfuls into my own mouth, severely burning my tongue. I gulped water and tried to pace myself, but I was more or less out of control.

"So, are you almost finished with your novel?" I asked. "Can you tell me that much?"

Her mouth turned down at the corners and she dabbed it with her napkin. "Soon, I think. The ending is difficult. I want to get every word right."

"I know just what you mean! Sometimes I change a line so many times I can't remember how it started out. I feel like there's an exact way to say what I want to say, but I haven't found it yet." We were so much alike, I thought. Maybe we *could* be "us."

"Yes!" she said. "The difference between the right word and the almost right word is like the difference between . . ." She paused a minute, and I knew she would come up with a perfect simile. "The difference between lightning and a lightning bug."

And it was funny, too! "Yes! Oh, you nailed it!"

We grinned at each other. She took another sip of her margarita and pushed it across the table to me. I drank the magic potion.

"You may be only eighteen, but you're a writer already, Marisol," Olivia said. "You understand the way in which words can change their meanings right in front of you. The way they pick up flavors and odors like butter in a refrigerator."

There was something about the way she was staring at me that made me hold my breath. My insides began to feel like butter that had been *out* of the refrigerator for a long, long while. Butter in a pan, on a hot stove. I dropped my fork as she glided from her chair into the one next to me. She put one hand behind my head and brought my face close to hers. And kissed me. Kissed me hard. And every other thought went out of my head except *Olivia*.

After that it seemed like only a few minutes before we were at her apartment, in her bedroom, me drunkenly pulling at her sweater, her smoothly removing my clothes. Then, as I watched, she slipped off her skirt, pulled the sweater over her head, and pushed me backward onto the bed.

I seemed to be waiting an excruciatingly long time to feel her mouth again. And, in the meantime there was a moaning noise coming from my own mouth and a tremendous feeling of happiness or nervousness or a combination of both making my limbs tremble uncontrollably.

And then her mouth was on me again, on every part of me, and I knew I was dying of love.

CHAPTER FIFTEEN

THE MARGARITAS WERE BEGINNING to wear off by midnight, when Olivia brought me a tall glass of water.

"Drink this, baby. So you don't feel hung over tomorrow." I sat up in her bed and watched as she pulled on a pair of jeans and a hooded sweatshirt—even in those she looked fantastic. Why did there have to be a tomorrow? It certainly couldn't be an improvement on tonight, in which I was Olivia's "baby."

"Where are you going?" I asked.

"Where are *we* going, you mean. I'm taking you home."

"Why?"

"Because I like to wake up in the morning by myself," she said, as she slipped into her shoes. "Drink that now, and get dressed."

I guess my feelings must have been splashed all over my face. Olivia looked up and laughed, gently. "Oh, Marisol, don't be hurt. It's just the way I am. Besides, we can't arrive together at the class in the morning. If the other students got wind of this, they would think I favor you. Which I obviously do." She came to the bedside and leaned over to kiss me again, except this time the kiss felt a little bit hurried and purposeful.

I drank the water and climbed out of bed to search for my scattered clothing.

"I'll check my e-mail while you dress, but hurry, please, sweetheart," she said. "I need to get some sleep tonight."

Sweetheart. Baby. That was *me.* I pretended to be drowsy on the ride back to my apartment so I wouldn't have to say much. This had been the most amazing day and night of my life—my whole body was still quivery and vulnerable with emotion. I would have been ecstatic if only that grain or two of salt hadn't found its way into my open wound of a heart. After the way Olivia had stroked and petted and *loved* me, how could she want me out of the way so she could go to sleep and wake up by herself? I wanted nothing more than to wake up next to her!

It occurred to me that I was probably not the first student who'd been in love with Olivia Frost. Of course we were all awed by her. Maybe she bought amber pendants by the truckload. And how in the hell were you supposed to know what the other person felt at a time like this? It was hard enough to decipher your own feelings!

But when the car pulled up at my building, Olivia pulled me close, and I could feel her heart beating as quickly as mine. She kissed me again, nipping softly at my lips, then pulled away. "Until tomorrow, love."

I staggered up the stairway and put myself to bed once again. She'd called me love. *Love, love, love.* What did that mean? There was no chance in hell I was going to sleep a wink.

Which is why Google was invented, right? For insomniac stalkers who need more information immediately. I typed in

"Olivia Frost," and there they were: 589 entries. None of them, or so it seemed, *my* Olivia Frost.

First a genealogy site came up, then an Olivia Frost who had spoken at the 2004 Tourism in Kansas conference, then Edith Olivia Frost, a renowned rose gardener. No, no, no. And not Olivia Frost the women's ice hockey star at the University of Delaware, either. Not the wine exporter, the folk singer, or the vice-president of branding and marketing development for something called INSIG. God, who'd have thought there were so many Olivia Frosts in the world? There were several in the UK and one each in Sweden and Japan.

And then, finally, I got a hit: Olivia Frost, assistant editor, *Harvard Review*. Harvard—that had to be her. I clicked through to the site and scanned it until I found her name. I jumped in my seat just looking at it. Three years ago Olivia Frost had been the assistant editor of the magazine, but there was no more information than that. The *Harvard Review* was apparently a literary magazine, run by the university, which published writers whose names I mostly didn't recognize. However, the names I did recognize, John Updike and Adrienne Rich, made me think it was probably a pretty prestigious publication.

Olivia would have already graduated from Harvard three years ago—they must have hired her for the staff. Because she was brilliant, obviously. What magazine wouldn't want someone with her brains on its editorial staff? If only there were pictures on the website, I could go to see her whenever I wanted to! I read every bit of information on the website and then spent another hour on the genealogy pages.

At eight o'clock the next morning I was slumped over the

newspaper at the kitchen table, slugging down a bowl of black coffee, Peaches curled in my lap, when Birdie came through the front door with Noodles. As soon as he let her off the leash, she dashed into the kitchen and put her paws on my lap, begging to be allowed to slather my face with slime. I declined the invitation, but Peaches let her get in a few good slurps.

"Down, Noody," I said. "Down, honey. Your claws need to be clipped."

"You look like shit," Birdie said, walking into the kitchen.

"Thank you, Tyra Banks."

"What time did you get back last night? Did you go to *her* place?"

"I got back late," I said, avoiding the second question. "You and the wife were already in bed."

Birdie poured himself a cup of coffee and took a sip. "Lord, could this be any stronger?" He screwed up his face and tossed the liquid into the sink. "You might as well just eat the grounds out of the bag."

"I needed it strong. I couldn't sleep."

"I'd never sleep again, if I drank this crap every day." He gave me a coy look. "So, what happened?"

"We went to Zócalo for dinner."

"And . . ."

"We drank some margaritas."

"And . . ."

"We went back to her place."

Birdie put his hand on his hip. "Don't make me beg you. I want details."

I sighed. "Okay. I slept with her. But don't make a big deal of—"

Birdie's hug practically knocked my chair over. The animals scattered. "Oh, my God! Not only have you finally vanquished your virginity, but you did it with that totally hot chick!"

I laughed. "Yeah, I guess I did."

"Well, let's celebrate! Let's eat something really bad for us!"

"I can't. I have to take a shower and get to class," I said.

Birdie drew in a long breath. "And you'll see her again! And she'll sneak little looks at you and you'll have this great secret and no one else in the class will know! I'm loving it!"

"I know. I give you permission to celebrate without me."

Birdie's excitement had reignited my own. I had actually been with Olivia last night. There had been some spectacular losing of so-called innocence, and who knew what might happen next? So Olivia wasn't big on the romantic morning-after stuff; at least the night before had been unforgettable. As I sailed down the hallway, I passed Damon stumbling in the other direction. "Are there any doughnuts in the kitchen?" he asked hopefully.

"Oh, if only you'd told me you wanted some," I said, brushing the arm of his fleece bathrobe tenderly. "I'd have waved my fairy wand!"

He brushed his hair from his eyes and stared at me.

"Is she in a good mood?" I heard him ask Birdie.

"Incredible, isn't it?" Birdie said. "I think we owe Cupid a round of applause."

***

By the time I got to Brattle Street, I was a wreck. Even though the weather was much cooler than it had been, and I'd been more than generous with my deodorant, my T-shirt was still pitted out. Man, I could have used a couple of those margaritas before class.

"Marisol!"

Gio was sprinting to catch up to me. "I thought I'd be late. The T took forever this morning."

"Really?" I said, barely looking at him, thinking about walking into class and seeing Olivia Frost sitting there, her perfect legs crossed one over the other, wearing something silky that matched her extravagant hair.

"You okay?" he asked. "You look a little strange. Are you sick?"

"Just tired," I said, probably unconvincingly. "Did you write about Provincetown?" I asked, to throw him off the trail.

"Yeah. I was surprised how much I remembered. Details about the way things looked and smelled. I set a scene on the breakwater and had the characters arguing. So they're walking along this beautiful but precarious stone bridge while they're trying to sort out their confusing relationship. I hope it works."

"Oh, that sounds good," I said honestly. "We should talk again. About writing, I mean."

He nodded. "Yeah, I'd like to. I can have lunch today if you want."

"Okay, let's."

And then there was nothing else to do but enter the classroom and look at her, crossed, silky, extravagant.

Olivia glanced up at us as we walked in, but didn't give any indication that I was anyone special, a student she knew any better than the others. I was disappointed that Birdie's prediction wasn't coming true, but I knew Olivia wanted to be careful about this. After all, everybody in the class was probably crazy about her. Well, everybody except Gio. Still, having the secret was so exciting, I wasn't sure I'd be able to act normally, speak in my usual voice, hide my smile.

Several students read the scenes they'd written during the week. The first one, by Mandy, missed the mark altogether. She had her characters sitting on a porch, which she described in as much detail as a home decorating magazine. They sat against Ralph Lauren pillows "with tiny elephants embroidered all over them" and talked about how they had always wanted to work in a zoo. I guess the elephant pillows and the zoo were connected somehow, but it didn't come through. Olivia gently explained to Mandy what was interesting about the piece and what didn't work.

The second writer to read was Cassandra Washington, the woman who "just knew" she could write, and her piece was not bad at all. She wrote about a long-married couple whose house had begun to resemble them, or vice versa. I wasn't sure exactly what the point was, but the writing was strong.

And then Gio read, and his piece was really good. The tension between the two characters built skillfully the farther they walked into the ocean on the uneven stone path, until they reached the point where they could go no farther, and their arguing stopped and so did their relationship. I thought it was the best thing of his I'd ever heard, and I waited, almost proudly, to hear what Olivia would say.

Her blank face revealed nothing. "That was clever," she said. "A little obvious, though, don't you think? The bumpy road of life?"

Gio looked pale. "Well, I—"

"Of course, a lot of people like cleverness," she continued. "I just think you could have tried a little harder to come up with something unique." She turned to the class, and then to me. "What do you think, Marisol?"

"Me? Well, I liked it. Especially the way the couple got angrier and angrier as the rocks got more slippery and harder to walk on."

"And yet, the piece doesn't make a very subtle point, does it?" Olivia stared straight into my eyes.

I didn't know what to say. I felt like she was telling me what to think. The whole class, everyone but Gio, was staring at me, waiting to see if I'd dare to disagree. Finally I stuttered, "Well, I don't know. I guess it could have been more subtle."

It was close enough to agreement; Olivia smiled her approval. "John, you obviously understood the assignment, but I do feel you've taken the easy way out. Next time, put a little more effort into it, okay?"

Gio nodded, but he looked depressed. He *had* put effort into it—I knew that. And even the two pieces before his, the lousy one and the mediocre one, hadn't gotten such a personal thrashing from Olivia. I decided it must be because she knew he was actually a better writer than they were and she was challenging him. At lunch I'd tell him that.

In a few more minutes, after Hamilton Hairdo and Mary

Lou were finished, it was my turn to put my neck on the block. After what had happened to Gio, I was worried. What if she laid into me like that? I wouldn't know what to say afterward. It occurred to me that this was a good reason not to date your teacher. Too late now. I took a deep breath and read.

When I looked up from the paper, Olivia was beaming. "Now *that's* what I was looking for! That was brilliant, Marisol!"

Brilliant? Really?

"I want you to read it again, and this time I want the rest of you to really listen to the way in which this piece works, how it grabs your emotions on so many levels—the demise of the building, the tree, maybe even life as Christina knows it. And yet change is relentless, whether for better or worse. I'm so impressed!"

The rest of the class stared at me again, some looking merely glum, others obviously pissed off that I was in the spotlight again. Gio kept his eyes on the table.

After the second read-through, Olivia continued her praise, which was totally embarrassing. I was sure no one knew what had happened between us, but I felt sleazy anyway. I mean, I thought my piece was pretty good, but was it really that much better than the others? That much better than Gio's? I wanted to feel I could trust Olivia to tell me the truth about my writing, but now I wasn't sure.

"Next week we'll be talking about plotting. I want you to think about an incident you usually avoid remembering, or a time you felt really frightened or defeated. Or think of a fight you may have witnessed between two people you love. What lay behind these events? What is their meaning? Can you get a story out of it? Remember, the role of a writer is not to say what we all can say, but what we are unable to say."

Everyone shuffled out the door quickly the moment class was dismissed. Nobody said a word to me.

"Can I meet you outside?" I said to Gio. "I just want to talk to her for a minute."

Gio glanced at Olivia and then back to me. "Sure," he said, and I wondered if he was figuring out the whole situation.

The minute the classroom was empty, Olivia walked over to me and put her arm around my waist. "Hello there, my star," she said. "I was hoping you'd stick around a few minutes."

Her touch on my back was enough to render me momentarily speechless, but I struggled to get the words out.

"I wanted to talk to you about what you said about my piece. Did you really like it that much?"

She laughed and cocked her head so that her hair drifted from her shoulder onto mine. "Would I lie to you?"

"No, I didn't mean that, but I wondered if you were exaggerating just a little. I mean, I didn't think mine was that much better than Gio's. I mean John's."

Olivia pulled her arm away from me. "You know him, don't you? From before this class, I mean."

"Well, yeah. We met last spring."

She nodded and smiled, enigmatically. "I thought so. You looked awfully cozy when you walked in together this morning, and you were talking to him at the Arts Festival, too. You've even got a nickname for him. Is this something I should know about?"

"What? No! We're just friends, and I was afraid he might get discouraged by what you said. It seemed kind of harsh."

She took another step away from me. "It's impossible to discourage the real writers—they don't give a damn what you say; they're going to write. And besides, you agreed with me, didn't you?"

"Well, no, not really. I thought it was a good piece of writing."

"Then you should have said that during class. I would have admired you for taking me on in front of the others, but whining about it after class is pretty cowardly, don't you think?" She sounded almost angry, and it scared me a little.

"You're right. I'm sorry. I don't know why I'm complaining about this now. I guess I just felt funny about how much you praised my work in front of everybody."

"I meant what I said, Marisol. Do you think I only praised you because . . ." She looked around the room as though suddenly worried she'd be overheard.

"No, I didn't think that. Don't be mad," I said. For a minute we just looked at each other like two sword fighters trying to guess where the other will strike, but then I could see Olivia calming down, and I relaxed a little.

"I'm not mad," she said, a crooked smile breaking on her face. "I suppose this is why teachers shouldn't fall for their students. The roles get confused."

Her easy admission that she'd fallen for me took my breath away, then made me brave. I stepped close and took her hand.

"Will I see you this week?" I asked her.

"I hope so. I have a lot of work to do, but I want to see you, too. I'll call you."

I nodded. "Okay. And, um, I guess I should tell you, I'm not going to be in class next Saturday. I'm going to Provincetown with some friends—we have a chance to stay in this amazing place, and—"

Olivia dropped my hand, and her face darkened. "Is this a joke? You're running off to Provincetown with somebody *else*? You're going with *him*, aren't you? That John?" Her eyes were sparking.

"No! I'm going with some friends—"

"You just said *he* was your friend."

"He is, but I'm going with Birdie and Damon. My roommates. You met them, remember?" It suddenly didn't seem like a good idea to mention that Lee was part of the traveling circus. If Olivia was jealous of Gio, the idea of me being in gay paradise with another lesbian was not going to please her.

She crossed her arms over her chest and hugged out her annoyance. "If I'd known you wanted to go to P'town, I'd have offered to take you. There's a guest house right on the water where I always stay."

"Well, we could go there together another time, couldn't we? Provincetown isn't going to disappear." I gave a little laugh, as if this had all been a silly misunderstanding.

I could tell she was trying—without complete success—to get her anger under control. "It's not a good idea to miss a class, either. Every class is a lesson," she said.

"I know that. I intend to do the assignment anyway." I

moved in close to her again. "Maybe the teacher will give me a private lesson?"

Olivia turned away from me and pretended to look for something in her bag. "The teacher does not like being blown off, Marisol." She sounded hurt.

"That's not what I'm doing!" I insisted.

"No? It feels like it."

"It isn't! I mean, I hardly even knew you when I made these plans . . ."

"Well, you know me now, don't you?" she said, turning to face me.

I wanted so badly to kiss her again, to make everything all right, but I didn't dare do it here where someone might see us.

"I *love* knowing you," I said, as close as I dared come to a declaration.

"Do you?" she asked, staring at me. For just that moment she looked completely unguarded, as if I could enter through her eyes and tumble into her soul.

Stunned, I said, "Of course I do. You know that."

She nodded and looked away. "Okay. I'll call you, then."

"Call me soon," I said as I backed toward the doorway. But she didn't turn around again.

When I got outside and saw Gio waiting, I panicked a little. I certainly didn't want Olivia to come out the door and find me standing there talking to my "friend," of whom she was already suspicious.

I grabbed Gio's arm, startling him. "Let's go!" I said. "I'll explain later." I pulled him around the corner and we kept running until we got to the Bombay Club.

Chapter Sixteen

O F COURSE GIO WANTED TO KNOW what the hell we were running away from, but I managed to sidetrack him for a while with deciding which window table was the best, and then with my thoughts about every entrée on the menu. Once we ordered, I segued into a monologue on Indian women's clothing, pointing out some of the lovely saris and other silk outfits that floated past us.

"I like those pajama-like things," I said. "But I watched somebody put on a sari one time. No way could I ever wrap myself up like that every day. A sari is really just one huge piece of material," I continued, giving him the details of the pleat and tuck technique as though I were the local sari-wrapping expert. Somehow I managed to keep up this patter until the food arrived. Unfortunately, I couldn't talk and eat at the same time.

"Don't think you're getting away without giving me an explanation for that hundred-meter dash through Harvard Square," Gio said as he dove into his chicken biryani.

I exhaled slowly. There was a lot I needed to talk to somebody about, and Gio was right here, willing to listen. If we were really going to be able to be friends, maybe this was the time to test it out.

"Here's the bottom line," I said, trying to sound matter-of-fact between spoonfuls of mulligatawny soup. "I'm dating Olivia. At least, I went to dinner with her this week and . . . things progressed." I pulled the amber pendant out from beneath my T-shirt. "She bought me this," I said, hoping the gift would reveal what I couldn't.

Gio stopped eating and stared, first at the pendant, then into my eyes.

"And she knows I know you," I blundered on, "and for some reason she's kind of . . . jealous or something. So, I didn't want her to see us leaving together."

He shook his head as if to get the information to line up straight. "So, when Diana and I ran into you at the Arts Festival—you were *with* her, weren't you?"

I nodded.

"I wondered at first if that's what was going on, but I convinced myself it wasn't, that you'd just bumped into her like we did."

"She doesn't want anyone to know; she wouldn't be happy if she knew I was telling you."

"Huh," he grunted, still staring at me as if trying to take in the changes. "She doesn't seem like your type."

The comment startled me and I laughed. "How the hell do you know what my type is? You thought *you* were my type." His eyes darkened and he glared at me. Okay, sometimes I am a tactless bitch.

"I'm sorry. I'm not trying to be mean," I said.

"I guess it just comes naturally to you," he countered.

I sighed. "Mea culpa! I'm assuming you thought she wasn't

my type because she's so gorgeous and I'm so . . . not."

Gio tried hard to keep his scowl working. "I hope you aren't fishing for compliments, Marisol, because you've really gotten me out of the mood for them."

I played with my soup, not looking at him. "Of course I'm not."

"I mean, I did once declare my love for you—idiot that I am—so presumably I find you relatively attractive."

"That's not what I meant." I thought it was a good thing that he could talk about it like that, without freaking out or anything, but jeez, it was freaking *me* out a little.

"All I'm saying is, you don't do yourself up like her, with the high fashion and the hairdo and everything. You're a more interesting person, and, frankly, a deeper person than she is. At least, I think so."

"Deeper? Are you kidding? Olivia is so smart—she knows so much—"

"I didn't say she wasn't smart. I just think, I don't know, for all her confidence and big education and everything, she isn't somebody I'd like to sit and have a conversation with."

"Why not?"

He hesitated. "She seems so competitive. Like she'd have to *win* the conversation."

I was slightly dumbfounded. "That's not true." I went back to my soup and slurped up a few more spoonfuls before asking, "So, you don't like her?"

He shrugged. "Maybe I'm not being fair. Maybe I'm still stung by what she said about my piece today."

Of course he was! I'd meant to talk to him about that.

"Your piece was good—it really was. I don't know what Olivia was thinking, being so hard on you. Maybe because you *are* a good writer, she wanted to challenge you or something."

He smirked. "And she didn't want to challenge *you*, the 'brilliant' one?"

I put my hands over my face. "I know, I know. That was so embarrassing."

"Well, at least now I get it. I mean, you know I always liked your writing, but Lord, she acted like the rest of us should just step back and hand you the Nobel Prize."

"Oh, so now you figure she only complimented me because we're seeing each other?" Not that the thought hadn't occurred to me, too.

"Well, maybe it isn't the *only* reason." Gio's eyes lit up. "Wait a minute . . . is that why she was so hard on me? She thinks there's something going on between us, and she wanted to humiliate me!"

"Oh, no, Gio, I don't think so. Olivia wouldn't do that!"

"You sure?"

I had to admit Olivia seemed to have a temper when she got upset—I'd just glimpsed it for the first time myself. I thought it over for a minute and decided to come clean with Gio about everything.

"To tell you the truth, Olivia is pissed off at me, too, right now. I told her I wasn't coming to class next Saturday, and she freaked out."

"How come you won't be there?"

"Because I'm going to Provincetown."

"You are? Because I'm going?"

"Boy, your confidence bounced right back, didn't it? *No*, I was planning to go before I knew you were going. I wasn't going to tell you at first, but what the hell? We'd probably run into each other in Butterfield's anyway."

He gave me a lopsided grin. "I guess you were afraid I'd weep and moan and rend my garments."

"I never know what you're going to do, Gio. And I wanted a fun weekend, not a drama festival."

Gio stared out the window as the waiter cleared the table. I ordered some coffee, but Gio declined with a shake of his head. Finally he turned back to me.

"I think I'm over you," he said. "The funny thing is, I'm not that happy about it. I mean, I want to move on and everything, but it was exciting to be with you. I know, I wasn't actually *with* you, but still, we had a good time."

I didn't know what to say. Nobody had ever announced it to me like that before: *I'm over you.* And the funny thing was, I wasn't that happy about it either, even though it was totally what I'd been hoping for. I mean, I certainly didn't want Gio to be mooning after me forever, but I guess the idea that he loved me wasn't all that abhorrent to me after all. It doesn't happen all that often that somebody tells you they love you. I guess you shouldn't take it for granted, even if you don't feel the same way about them.

"We can still have some good times, can't we? I mean, if you're *over* me, couldn't we just be friends? Or, are you so over me you can't stand the sight of me?"

He smiled. "No, I'm not *that* over you."

"So, what's the deal with Diana? That going okay?"

"Yeah, it is, actually."

I nodded. "Good. I like her. I mean, she's awfully *nice*, but then you're probably in the mood for somebody who's not a bitch this time around, huh?"

"It's a pleasant change. So, what's the deal on you going to P'town? Who are you going with?"

"Birdie and his new boyfriend, Damon." I rolled my eyes. "Damon drives me nuts, but since it was Birdie's mother who got us a free place to stay, I couldn't very well object. And this new friend of mine, Lee, is also going. She just came out to her family and moved here from the Midwest. She's having kind of a hard time, and I thought a weekend in P'town would cheer her up."

"*That's* why Olivia got mad—you're going with another woman!"

"I didn't even tell her that. She thought I was going with *you*."

"Oh, great! And when I don't show up for class either, she'll be sure of it. She'll never have a good word to say about anything I write again!"

God, she *would* think that. I'd have to buy her something in Provincetown, something to prove I was thinking of her. Or maybe I'd call her. She'd be mad, but I could fix it. Couldn't I?

"Hey, you know what?" Gio said. "We *could* all go down together. My dad's letting me drive his second car down because he's obviously thrilled that I'm seeing a woman who isn't a lesbian for a change. I wasn't sure I wanted to, because it's a big old gas-guzzler, but if there were five of us going it would still be a lot cheaper than taking the bus or the boat."

"Huh. It's an idea. You did hear the part about how Birdie is going?"

"Yeah. I was trying to ignore that."

"Birdie in the car for three hours is impossible to ignore."

"Noted."

"And Damon is more or less an imbecile, but that can be comic relief. I think you'd like Lee. She's quiet," I said, then laughed, "but deep."

"As deep as you?"

"Deeper. It's possible she's the Grand Canyon of deepness."

"Well, hey, I'm in. As you know, deep lesbians are my thing."

We laughed too loud and the waiters turned to stare at us as we high-fived. Two geeky friends.

CHAPTER SEVENTEEN

I'D CALLED OLIVIA SEVERAL TIMES early in the week and left messages for her, but she didn't call back until Wednesday morning. She still sounded slightly aggravated, but we made plans to meet for a working lunch at Café Algiers.

I arrived before she did and set up my laptop. I intended to do the assignment as a scene between Christina and Natalie in which they disagree about something. Not so hard to imagine that at the moment. But what did they disagree about? I didn't want to mirror the truth too closely, because Olivia would obviously read it. I made a couple of false starts and had just come up with an idea I liked when Olivia appeared.

"I'm late, I know," she said. "Traffic was miserable."

"It's okay."

She nodded toward my computer. "I see you haven't missed me—you're typing away as usual."

"I thought you said we'd have a working lunch? Didn't you bring your laptop?"

"I didn't say that."

"Yes, you did. You said we'd work for an hour or so and then eat."

She drummed her ringed fingers on the tabletop. "These tables are too small to work at. Besides, I can't wait an hour to eat—I'm starving. We can go back to my apartment after lunch and work there. Doesn't that sound better?"

The mere mention of her apartment started my heart beating faster. Olivia's small studio held only a desk, a chair, and a bed. How likely was it that I'd get any work done in an environment that was permanently linked in my mind with sex? Of course, now that the notion of sex with Olivia was lodged in my mind, I started caring a lot less about working on my novel. I closed my laptop and we ordered lunch.

Once the food and coffee arrived, Olivia relaxed, and we talked and joked as we had the week before. By the time our order of baklava arrived, Olivia had hooked one of her legs around one of mine and was leaning across the table conspiratorially.

"How about we take the afternoon off and play?" she said. "You've already done some writing today, and I can afford a little vacation."

"Would this be a vacation in your apartment?" I asked.

"Well, we can't very well go to your apartment, can we? Between the dog and the dust, I'd have to be hospitalized."

My excitement was just slightly tempered by disappointment. Not that I didn't want to spend the afternoon "playing" at Olivia's—God, who wouldn't? It was just that work time with her was valuable to me too. I'd been looking forward to the work, the talking about the work, and *then* the playing. That was my idea of the perfect day.

But all it took was thirty seconds of Olivia staring into

my eyeballs to banish all thoughts of literary accomplishment. She left twenty dollars on the table, took my hand, and led me where she wanted me to go. Who could say no to Olivia?

She kissed me in the car, and on the stairs, and as she unlocked the apartment door. I was already lightheaded by then, but still managed to unbutton her blouse and hold her breasts in my hands so I could take a long look at them in the light of day. Flawless, just like everything else about her. Her breath quickened as I stroked them, and she said, "Oh, God, you do have the touch."

We made love more slowly than the first time, more luxuriously. Somehow it was even more exciting than the time before. I was beginning to know what excited her, and what excited me, too. And we were delighted to take each other to those places.

"You're a fast learner," Olivia said afterward, kissing my neck.

"You're a good teacher." That, however, must not have been the proper response: Olivia sat up in bed and looked at me.

"You haven't told anyone about this, have you?" she asked. "You aren't bragging about sleeping with the teacher, are you?"

"No!" I said, and then amended it. "Well, I did tell Birdie, but he doesn't know anybody to tell."

"Well, don't talk about it to anyone else, okay? I don't want to lose my job."

"I won't," I promised her, just before remembering that

LOVE & LIES

I'd also told Gio. I'd be sure to tell him not to mention it to anyone.

"I would never do anything to hurt you," I said, almost whispering the words.

Olivia smiled. "You're sweet. But you know, I've heard that before."

I felt like she'd smacked me. "Well, maybe those people *before* didn't love you!" The words were out before I'd thought through what I was saying.

"And you do?" she asked, as if she were only mildly curious.

I sat up too and pulled the blanket up around myself. "I . . . I don't know. Maybe I do."

She leaned over and kissed me gently. "Maybe you do. You're a sweet girl." She got out of bed, and I watched her perfectly shaped body walk away from me. "I need to take a shower. I have a dinner to go to later."

"Who are you going to dinner with?" I sounded like a petulant child even to myself.

"Just some colleagues," she said. "It's a Harvard thing. Don't worry about it."

"I'm not worried," I said as she disappeared into the bathroom.

I sat in the bed another minute, a blanket pulled up around me, paralyzed, listening to the shower come on. Why had I said that about *loving* her? The words had just flown out of my throat! God, she kept calling me "sweet" like I was some twelve-year-old girl with a crush! And what she *hadn't* said was worse than what she had.

Finally I got up and dressed, yanking the zipper on my

jeans so hard that it went off the track. It was as if I'd lost control of everything.

The shower was still running as I paced around the apartment, humiliated by my own impulsiveness. Which was when I noticed that Olivia's computer was on, its screensaver blinking a series of photographs across the screen. I pulled up the desk chair to look at them.

They seemed to be chronological, and Olivia was in them all. There was an adorable toddler who already had thick black hair, then a stubborn-looking grade-school girl, a breathtaking teenager in a bikini, and, finally, a picture of Olivia with her arms around a very handsome man that looked like it could have been taken in Harvard yard. I was surprised by that one at first, which seemed to be a portrait of a happy couple. But then I decided that no, the guy must be her brother. After all, both of them were better looking than 99 percent of the college students I'd ever seen.

I accidentally brushed the keyboard with my hand, and the screensaver photos dissolved into a menu page. I knew I shouldn't look at it, but it was hard not to—I craved information about Olivia, and there it was in front of me.

There were only a few folders listed in the menu, but one of them was called Lillian. The novel! I'd never thought of myself as sneaky before, but there it was, the book about which Olivia would tell me nothing except the title. Just a couple of clicks away. I could just take a peek. The shower was still running. I clicked.

At the top of the page in bold capital letters was the title: *LILLIAN, WHO SAYS SHE LOVES YOU*. Which of course reminded me that I had just said the same thing. I wondered if poor Lillian had felt as dumb afterward as I did. There was no chapter one or any other heading underneath the title. Instead, this seemed to be a series of notes about the character of Lillian.

—Hatred of her parents colors her life. She can never forgive their betrayal of her.

—Moves to the East Coast, hoping to leave her ghosts behind. At Harvard she is a brilliant student.

—So beautiful that everyone falls in love with her. They blur in her mind, one no different than another, all of them too privileged for their own good.

—She falls in love with everyone, and no one.

—Trusts no one but herself—the only way to be safe. Safety is being alone, with the door closed.

—No sadness. Lill is done with sadness. She intends to come out on top.

That was all that was written on the page. Interesting, as far as it went, but it only hinted at what the novel might actually be about. The notes about Lillian moving to the East Coast and being "so beautiful" pointed to an autobiographical element to the book, which made me feel better about my own story. If Olivia could do it, so could I. But the sentence that made me shiver was, "Safety is being alone, with the door closed."

I suspected it said more about who Olivia really was than she'd ever told me herself.

Guiltily, I clicked back to the menu page. Where, I wondered, were the chapters themselves? But before I could see what the other files were, the shower stopped.

What was I doing snooping around on Olivia's computer? She would be furious if she knew. I lowered the laptop case so she wouldn't see that the screensaver was gone, then got up and walked across the room. By the time she emerged from the bathroom, wrapped in terry cloth, I was sitting on the end of her bed staring blindly at a copy of *Film Comment* magazine I'd found on the floor.

I kept my eyes on the magazine while she dressed silently. Things were weird between us now, and I didn't know whose fault it was. Who was acting stranger, Olivia or me? There was only one more kiss to come my way that afternoon, at my front door, and it didn't tell me anything I wanted to know.

Sophie got the job at the bakery. They wanted her to start there right away, and Doug told her to go ahead, he'd figure out something. It was an easier job for her—only five mornings a week and only baking pies, no mixing up tuna salad or making meat loaf for the dinner crowd.

"I'll be done by noon," she told me. "Four hours of work a day is plenty for me; unfortunately, I'm not gettin' no younger either."

"I'm glad you got something good, Sophie," Doug said. "You earned it."

Sophie pressed her lips together tightly. "You know I'm

gonna miss this place, though. All these years of us being a team here. Seems a shame it's all over with, just like that." She snapped her fingers to show the speed of change.

"We'll still be here awhile longer. You can come visit us," Doug said with barely a trace of emotion in his voice. He was planning to retire once the Mug closed for good, and he acted like he was looking forward to it, but I knew he was actually having a hard time. I'd walked in on him when he was sitting on a box of tomato juice back in the storage room, making a gurgling sound in his throat and dabbing at his eyes with a chef's apron. I'd backed out quietly.

Pete, the short-order cook, was going to take some of Sophie's hours, but we wouldn't have a baker on site anymore—we'd be getting ready-made pies from a wholesaler.

"Place is going down the tubes," Sue, the early-shift waitress, said when I came in to relieve her on Thursday. "I'm gonna look for something in Boston. You?"

"I'll stay here until the Mug closes," I said. "Then I might just get temp work, you know, from an agency."

"Marisol is going to college next fall, aren't you, honey?" Sophie said, proud on my behalf, thinking she was coming to my rescue.

"Um, yeah."

Sue rolled her eyes. "If that's the case, why are you even working here in the first place?" She balled up her dirty apron and shoved it in the laundry hamper, then turned to leave before I could think of an answer. I could have said, "I have to pay rent too, you know." But in fact I didn't have to. My mother happily gave me all the money I needed. And Dad had offered to find me a paid internship at MIT too, but I hadn't wanted that. I wanted to move out of my parents' house and get my own job and write a novel. I wanted to get going on life, to grow up. But when I thought about people like Sue or Pete or even Sophie, I realized that choosing to grow up was a luxury, one they hadn't had.

Lee came in at three thirty as usual, and I joined her in her booth for a minute.

"So, are you getting excited about going to Provincetown?"

"I am," Lee said. "I looked it up on the Web. It says it's been a gay mecca for half a century. That's pretty cool."

"You won't believe this place," I assured her. "It'll make you glad you're gay."

She frowned. "I *am* glad I'm gay. Don't you think I am?"

"Well, you're not exactly the Gay Pride poster girl." Oh, man, was I stepping on her toes again? "Maybe it's just that you're depressed about having to leave Indiana."

"I didn't *have* to leave. I wanted to. They didn't buy me a bus ticket and say, 'Get outta town,' the minute I came out!"

"I didn't say that."

"I could have stayed. It's not like there aren't any gay people in Indiana, you know."

"I know," I said, but I wasn't sure I did. I wasn't at all clear about what lay between the East Coast and California. Who were all those people?

"No, you don't know," Lee said, obviously picking up on my ambivalence. Her voice got louder. "You think I'm a hick from Cowtown. You probably think everybody in the Midwest still rides around in stagecoaches and gets their mail from the Pony Express!"

"I do not! Why are you getting all pissed off?" I asked.

She sighed and sipped at her tea. "Sorry. I'm not pissed off. I'm just homesick. It's weird to live someplace where people don't know a damn thing about the place you grew up. Or *care*."

"That's not true," I said, because I felt I should.

"Oh, no? Tell me something about Indiana. Here's an easy question: What states border it?" Lee stuck her chin out, challenging me.

"Well, Ohio, for one," I said, pretty sure of that guess.

"What else?"

"Um, let's see. Iowa, right?"

She made that *you're wrong* beeping noise.

"Really? Not Iowa? Are you sure?"

She made the noise again.

"Okay, then, it must be Illinois."

"Lucky guess. Two more to go."

"Really? Two?" I tried to picture a map of the United States, but I was drawing a big blank on that whole middle part.

"Maybe Wisconsin?"

Beep.

"Minnesota?"

Beep.

What the hell else was up there? "North Dakota?"

"Okay, you lose. You're not even close. It's Michigan to

157

the north and Kentucky to the south. Which just goes to show that your geography skills are lousy and that nobody in the East gives a damn about the Midwest."

"Oh, come on. I'm willing to learn! Especially now that I know there are gay people all the way out in those boondock states too. *The virus has spread!*" I said, trying to get her to laugh.

Which worked, sort of. She snorted and then looked away, reluctant to let me cheer her up completely. Well, if I couldn't, I had an idea who could.

"Hey, you should come with me to dinner tomorrow night at my parents' place. Home cooking to chase away homesickness. Not that my mother cooks, but at least it will be cooked in her home. Besides, they'd like to meet you. Well, Mom would, and Dad will be cordial anyway."

"Really?" She looked skeptical.

"I told you my mother is a total gay-rights cheerleader. She's probably planning my wedding ceremony already—you know, a cake with two brides, a gift certificate for a sperm donor . . ."

Lee shook her head. "Amazing. Sure, I'll go. Then I'll have even more proof for my claim that you are the luckiest person I know."

CHAPTER EIGHTEEN

FRIDAY AFTERNOON SOPHIE GAVE ME a big weepy hug before she left, and I had to work at not bawling myself. It was odd how you could get so close to people you didn't even know very well just because you worked together. In four months the Mug had begun to seem like a huge part of my life. It was odd; when I was in high school, everything revolved around school or home, and that was about it. Of course, I met Gio, and later Diana, through my zine-writing, but they were high-school kids too. Now my world had gotten so much larger: a job, an apartment, an incredible (if sometimes puzzling) girlfriend. So far I was a real fan of this growing-up stuff.

Lee was waiting for me in the pit after work. "So, was this Sophie's last day?"

I nodded. "I feel kind of sick."

"Because you had to say good-bye to her?"

"Because I had three pieces of her lemon meringue pie."

"Three!"

"I had to! When will I ever have it again?"

"I thought you said she'd be working at—"

"It won't be the same!" I yelled.

She put her hand on my arm. "I think you're having a sugar meltdown. Let's go get some protein at your parents' house."

"I can never eat again."

My mother threw open the door and grabbed me in her usual engulfing way. I introduced Lee, and Mom smothered her, too. Oops, I'd meant to warn Lee about that. She knew now. Dad showed up behind Mom and kissed me on the forehead, then politely shook hands with Lee.

"So, Marisol tells me you just moved here from Illinois!" Mom said as she ushered us into the living room, which she insisted on referring to as "the parlor."

Lee smiled, and I ducked my head. "Indiana, actually. I've been here about six weeks."

Mom grabbed her hand. "Well, we hope you'll love it here and decide to stay. This is a very supportive community for gays and lesbians. And I think there's a gay-straight alliance at your high school, Rindge and Latin, isn't there?"

Lee was a bit taken aback at how rapidly Mom had gotten to the point; she shot me a quick look of surprise. Of course none of it surprised me.

"Yeah, there is," Lee said. "I haven't joined it, though. I mean, I don't really know those kids."

Mom thought that over. "My friend Madeleine's son goes to Rindge—he must be in the GSA. Let me call her and find out about it for you. You should meet Theo anyway—he can introduce you to everyone. The GSAs around here are very vital, very active." She was on a roll. "Do you think your parents would be interested in getting some materials from PFLAG? I certainly don't want to force this on them, but if you think it might be . . ."

On and on she went. Saving people: her life's work. I could see Lee's initial hesitations melt away; before long she and my mother were old buddies. Mom even got her to promise to ride on the PFLAG float in the Pride parade next spring.

"Unless, of course, by that time you're involved with some other gay organization and you'd rather ride with them. I would completely understand that," Mom said, smiling.

As we walked into the dining room, Lee whispered in my ear. "Your mother is so cool!"

"I know," I said, but in truth I forgot it sometimes.

Over salmon patties and baked squash Mom continued to shine her high beams on Lee. "Now, tell me again where you two met?"

"Marisol and me? I came into the Mug, where she works. We just started talking one day."

"Well, that's not terribly romantic, is it? We'll have to come up with a better story than that. I'm thinking you met down by the Charles River during the annual regatta. Marisol was sitting under a tree, reading, but she couldn't help noticing when you—"

"Mom!" I interrupted. "You're jumping to conclusions! Lee and I aren't dating each other—we're just friends."

Her smile deflated. "Oh, dear. I thought, when you said . . ."

Dad, however, looked relieved. "Helen, I don't know why you insist on trying to push Marisol into dating. She'll find someone when she's ready."

"I wasn't pushing. I just thought—"

"Actually, Marisol *has* been seeing someone," Lee said. "Haven't you? The woman who bought you the necklace?"

"You have?" Mom said. "You're seeing someone and you didn't tell me?"

"Mom, it's not a big deal. I went out to dinner once or twice. I don't report it to you every time I eat a meal with somebody."

"You don't?" She actually looked crushed. This is the downside to having a cool and involved mother. She thinks she's cool enough to be involved in every single thing you do.

"Well, what's her name?" Mom wanted to know. "What's she like?"

"Her name is Olivia. She's a . . . teacher."

"A teacher? So, she's older than you."

"A little older, yes."

"Have you met her, Lee?"

"No, Marisol keeps her away from me, too," Lee said.

"I don't 'keep her away' from anybody. I've only gone out with her a few times. I don't know why we're even talking about this."

"You can't blame your mom for being curious," Lee said. "It seems strange to me, too, that you never want to talk about this Olivia person."

"When there's something to tell, I'll tell you. I'll tell everybody! I'll take out an ad in the *Boston Globe*!" I forked a big chunk of salmon into my mouth and took out my anxiety by masticating it to pulp.

"Well, I certainly hope Olivia is as nice a person as you

are," Mom said, reaching over to squeeze Lee's hand. "You're just the kind of daughter-in-law I'd love to have someday!"

After which Lee was careful not to look at me, I was careful not to look at her, and my father was careful not to look at anyone.

I got home at about nine thirty to an empty apartment. It took me ten minutes to get my stuff ready for the weekend in P'town, and by ten o'clock I was in bed, covers up, lights out, brooding. Partly about that daughter-in-law remark—God!—which had made everyone but my mother highly uncomfortable, but mostly because tomorrow morning Olivia would see that Gio and I were both absent from her class and would probably be angry with me again. Which were more difficult, relationships with friends, family, or lovers? Or did I just suck at all kinds of relationships?

Even gnawing on my poor fingernails wasn't calming me down, so I finally got up and turned on the light. I could work on my assignment for tomorrow's class, even though I wouldn't turn it in until the following week. *An incident I usually avoid remembering, or a time I felt really frightened or defeated. Or a fight I witnessed between two people I loved. And what lay behind these events.*

The minute I sat down at the computer, the cat leaped into my lap; I had to admit that Birdie's furry creatures had wormed their way into my affections pretty quickly. Peaches turned in a circle three times and settled down on my bathrobe, completely nonjudgmental about my ability to write a novel, or get a girlfriend, or pay the rent. Her steady purr began to relax me.

163

One of the best things about writing was being able to go into another space, far back into my brain, where the unthought thoughts lived. I let real life sink into the background and tried to become Christina. The idea of witnessing a fight appealed to me, but rather than use my own memories, I really wanted to try to incorporate the idea into my book. What if Christina witnessed a fight between two people she loved? Who were they? What would the circumstances be?

One of the combatants could be Natalie, but who was she arguing with, and why? After a minute of sitting there, watching Natalie and waiting, another woman appeared in my mind, someone who had a lot to say to Natalie. I started to imagine them talking, and I wanted to write it down, but the second woman needed a name. When I realized the second woman was Dorothy (aka my mother), the writing came in a flood.

"My daughter means more to me that anyone on earth," Dorothy said. "And I will *not* let anyone hurt her."

"Why do you think I would hurt her? Can you read the future?" Natalie said.

"No, but I can see the present, and when I look into your eyes, I don't see love."

Christina walked in with the second bottle of wine just in time to hear this accusation. "Mom, stop it! You don't know what you're talking about!"

"Christina isn't a child, Dorothy," Natalie

said. "You can't tell her who she's allowed to play with anymore. She's an adult."

"She's not as experienced as you are—she's never been in love. She doesn't understand that people can be cruel to each other!"

"I don't know why you're saying these things," Christina told Dorothy. "I trust Natalie completely." She poured more wine for Natalie and for herself.

"Do you think she loves you?" Dorothy said.

"Now you're the one who's being cruel," Natalie said. "I talk about my feelings when I'm alone with Christina—not in front of her mother!"

But Dorothy kept her eyes on Christina. "Do you?" she repeated.

"Yes," Christina said at last. "Natalie loves me and I love her." Her hand shook as she raised her wineglass.

Natalie smiled at her across the table. "We belong together," she said.

"I doubt it," Dorothy said sadly, as she refilled her own glass. "But I don't know how to stop you."

Wow, I hadn't seen that coming. I'd never heard my mother say anything like that to anyone before, and she'd never met Olivia, so where was this coming from? It was a weird variation on our dinner-table scene earlier. Very strange, but I liked the tension the scene was setting up, so I kept going and wrote another scene in which Christina and Natalie were back in Natalie's apartment. Although Christina dismissed her mother's predictions earlier, now she starts to worry. But when she presses Natalie for reassurance, Natalie becomes angry with her.

And when I wrote this line for Natalie, "'I would have admired you more if you didn't believe every word your mother says,'" I could hear Olivia's anger behind it. Which was really freaky. I had to remind myself I was making up these characters; they weren't actually Olivia and my mother and me.

A key turned in the apartment door, and Birdie and Damon burst in in their usual boisterous manner.

"Get a towel from the bathroom," Birdie ordered. "She's dripping all over everything."

"So am I!" Damon said. "I'm drying my own hair first."

I knew there was music to be faced with Birdie, which should be gotten out of the way before tomorrow morning, so I opened my door and stepped out.

Birdie stood on the small mat in front of the door holding Noodles as she shook herself violently.

"Is it raining?" I asked.

Birdie's own hair was matted to his head and water dripped into his eyes. He raised one eyebrow but didn't bother answering the question.

"Sorry. It was fine when I got home," I said.

"It's been pouring for twenty minutes. Which is exactly how far from home we were when it started." He looked toward the bathroom. "Bring a towel for me, too, Damon. Sometime this millennium."

Damon stalked back into the living room with a towel wrapped tightly around his own head, tossed another towel to Birdie, and threw the third one on top of the drenched doggie.

"Oh, thanks, Damon," I said. "You give *my* towel to the dog."

"I just grabbed what was hanging there."

I got down on my knees to dry Noodles, since the boys were busy with themselves. She licked me in gratitude, or maybe so I could be as wet as the rest of them. "So, is your mom coming over to take care of the animals this weekend?"

"Yes," Birdie said, his voice muffled by terry cloth. "Speaking of which!" He pulled the towel down and turned to glare at me. "What is that note you left me? We're riding down to the Cape with *Gio*? You invited him on our trip?"

"No! He was going down anyway to visit his new girl-friend in Truro. So get that I-told-you-so look off your face. His dad loaned him this big car, and it just makes sense for us to all go together. With five of us sharing gas it'll be cheaper than the bus. And more fun, too."

"Oh, yes, *fun*! Because we're all such good friends."

"Birdie, you hardly even know Gio. You were in a jealous snit last spring because you didn't have a boyfriend. You wanted to spend every minute with me, and I wanted to spend time with Gio. It'll be much different now. And Gio certainly won't be interested in Damon."

"Why not?" Damon said, looking hurt.

"I mean, he won't be interested in you romantically. He's straight," I explained.

"He's straight," Birdie repeated, "but he likes lesbians."

"He doesn't like 'lesbians.' He likes *me*," I said, then amended that. "He *liked* me. Past tense."

"Do you know for a fact there's a new girlfriend?" Birdie asked.

"Yes, Birdie. I know her."

"So, he's not staying with us, right?"

"No, he's staying with Diana. In Truro."

"And I won't have to sit up front with him, will I? In case he has cooties."

I sighed. "No, douche bag, I'll sit up front."

Then another possibility occurred to him, and he poked his finger toward me. "Is Olivia coming?"

"Is Olivia that beautiful woman?" Damon asked, looking back and forth between us.

"Yes, she's beautiful; no, she isn't coming. Lee's coming, and she and Olivia don't seem like a good match," I said.

"Ooh, keeping secrets from the girlfriend already! Not a good sign!" Birdie taunted, shaking his head.

"Who's Lee?" Damon wanted to know.

"Keep up, D.," Birdie reprimanded him. "You've met her. Baby dyke. Nice hair, good teeth."

"Won the Preakness last year," I said, thereby totally confusing the baffled Damon.

Birdie pretended to think. "You know, Lee seems more like the kind of person you usually hang out with. I mean, I can't really imagine your fabulous new girlfriend stuffed into the backseat of Gio's crummy car for three hours."

"I don't think it's crummy; it's his father's."

"Whatever. Olivia just seems too chic for your usual crowd."

"Believe me," I told him, "I'm considering tossing a few people out of my 'usual crowd' as we speak."

He shrugged. "Okay, okay. Don't be snotty—I'm letting your ex-boyfriend drive me to Provincetown."

"We're all thrilled," I said, tossing the damp, smelly dog towel in his face.

CHAPTER NINETEEN

EVEN THOUGH I'D TOLD BIRDIE the ride down with Gio would be fun, I actually had more than a few misgivings about it. There were too many variables: Was Gio a decent driver, and if not, could I wrest the wheel from him before Birdie started to crab about it? Would Lee feel uncomfortable around these three guys she didn't really know, who could all be odd in their own not-so-charming ways? Would the car be funereally quiet except for those moments when Birdie was embarrassing the hell out of me? And, worst of all, what if Gio's visit to Diana's turned sour and I ended up babysitting a bummed-out guy all weekend? All five of us had personalities that could be rough around the edges; what were the chances we'd have a great time all together?

And yet it certainly seemed like we were going to. My roommates and I picked up Lee at her apartment and then caught the T over to Back Bay, where Gio had the car ready to go. It was awkward at first, because Birdie reminded me within everybody's earshot that he was *not* sitting up front, and then before I could sit there myself, Damon plunked himself down in the shotgun seat and Birdie yelled at him to "get in the back of the bus with the other homosexuals."

Obediently Damon crawled back out and let me get in the front passenger seat, but not before I shot Birdie a look of disgust. Somehow excitement about the weekend was enough to get us past these initial stupidities, and we settled into the car. Gio stopped at a Dunkin' Donuts before we got on the highway, and the caffeine and sugar pumped up the excitement level even higher. When Damon yelled, "Road trip!" in his best Keanu-Reeves-wasted-on-pot voice, even I did not scoff.

As we lumbered down the highway, Gio asked Lee where she was from, and she told him. When he said he'd been to Indiana many times because his grandparents lived on a farm there, the girl began to honest-to-God *glow*. She leaned as far up into the front seat as the seat belt would allow, and they traded stories about riding on tractors and detasseling corn, whatever that meant. It turned out Gio had a whole bunch of relatives who didn't live far from the place where Lee grew up, and her high school played against his cousins' high school in sports, blah, blah, blah. Lee had a story about sitting out in a soybean field in August looking for shooting stars that had Gio howling with laughter. I didn't get it either, but when Birdie said, "What the hell are they talking about?" I didn't chime in. Obviously, if I got tired of sitting in the front seat, Lee would be happy to take my place.

Right around ten o'clock I had a few moments of agony imagining Olivia walking into the classroom at the Center and seeing both me and Gio missing. She would be thinking I'd lied to her and she'd be . . . what? Hurt? Angry? But surely I'd be able to explain everything, eventually. She couldn't stay mad forever at someone who had announced her love in such an adorably awkward way, could she?

I was still embarrassed about that, but I was starting to think, *What the hell?* It was the truth! When I thought of the anemic feelings I'd had for Kelly, my supposed "first girl-friend," they were just little puffs of smoke I'd been eager to fan into some flaming passion. But it had never really caught fire for either of us, which I hadn't entirely realized until Olivia appeared and my emotions leaped to fiery heights I hadn't known existed. When you feel that way, you want to tell the other person—it's only natural! And having sex with Olivia only made me love her more, because it made the whole thing feel real, like a grown-up emotional experience, not just some kid crush. I knew that no matter what happened down the line, I would never forget Olivia.

Gio turned out to be a good driver, for which I was grateful. He was careful and didn't take dumb chances, but he could also put the pedal to the floor when the situation called for it. Meanwhile Birdie started singing old Madonna songs in that way he has where you can't tell if he really likes the music or is just making fun of it. Damon joined in too, but without the irony. I got them to shut up by reading some poetry by my new favorite poet, James Merrill, who writes incredibly complicated poems about contacting angels and spirits through a Ouija board.

"That guy is great! Write down his name and the names of his books," Gio said. "I want to get them."

"There are bookstores in P'town. I bet we can find them there," I said.

"We're *not* going to Provincetown to look in *bookstores,*

for God's sake!" Birdie piped up. "You can do that anywhere!"

"Maybe Diana has them," Gio said. "She has a lot of poetry."

Which reminded me that we weren't all necessarily going to be hanging out together all weekend. Of course Gio would be with Diana. That was the only reason I'd even been willing to come down here with him—because he *wasn't* going to be hanging around with me. And now, suddenly, I was feeling kind of bad about that. I was remembering how much I'd enjoyed spending time with him, until it had gotten all complicated by sex—or the lack of it.

Wouldn't it be great if we all had a sex switch that we could turn off and on? So that you could hang out with somebody you liked as a friend and there would be no hurt feelings or sexual misunderstandings? I could turn mine on with Olivia and off around Lee and Gio. I guess the trick would be getting them to turn their switches off too.

We were hungry again by the time we got over the bridge and onto Cape Cod, so Gio pulled into a clam shack, the kind of place that has a three-foot lobster hanging over the doorway and seagulls circling the roof waiting for scraps.

As we crunched up to the take-out window, Lee said, "Are we walking on shells?"

"Yeah. More shells than dirt on Cape Cod," I said.

Lee looked around her at the scrubby pine trees and the sandy paths that ran off into the woods. She took a deep breath. "Wow. I can't see the ocean yet, but I can smell it. It's so beautiful out here."

"Just wait," I said. "You ain't seen nothin' yet."

"Thank you, Marisol," she said, smiling. "For bringing me here. And, well, for everything."

"You're welcome. I'm glad you're having a good time."

"I am. I really am."

The breeze was blowing her curls around, and she was holding her zippered sweatshirt closed with one hand while the other one hid in her back pocket. She looked very pretty, and it occurred to me that it was because she was happy. Maybe I'd never seen her really happy before.

Lee balked at ordering a clam roll, even though I raved about their local goodness, but Gio and I both got them, and everybody else, including Lee, ordered lobster rolls. We took our food to a picnic table and dug in.

"Oh my God, these are the best belly clams I've ever had," Gio said.

I nodded in agreement. "Onion rings aren't bad either."

"Fries good too," Damon mumbled as he stuffed a handful into his mouth.

"Tell us about it after you swallow," Birdie said, rolling his eyes. If *I'd* said that, Birdie would have cut me down like a tree.

Gio picked out a particularly fat clam from his roll and held it out to Lee. "Come on. You have to try one—you're on Cape Cod! There is nothing in the world like a perfectly fried belly clam."

Lee looked worried. "It's that word 'belly' that freaks me out," she said. "I'm a midwestern girl. I like meat loaf and an ear of corn."

"Trust me. My mother grew up in Coopersville, Indiana! Would I lie to you?"

Hesitantly, Lee took the food from his fingers and dared a small bite. "Ooh, it *is* good," she said, and popped the rest in her mouth. "Mmm. I'll never doubt you again, farm boy!"

Gio laughed and picked out another clam. "Told ya. Open up!"

She opened her mouth like a baby bird and let Gio feed another clam right into it. Quietly appalled, I watched them giggle. Oh my God, their car rapport was one thing, but feeding her by hand? Gio was doing it again! Didn't this guy learn from his mistakes?

After we polished off the food, we took turns visiting the tiny restrooms. I made sure to corner Gio the minute Lee was out of sight.

"What are you doing?" I asked him.

"What do you mean?" All innocence.

"I mean the giggling and the flirting and the dropping of food into Lee's mouth! She's a lesbian too, Gio!"

He laughed. "I know that. Believe me, I'm not as stupid as I was six months ago."

"No? You could have fooled me!" I sounded angry even to myself.

He gave me a funny look. "What are you getting all bent out of shape for? I like Lee, that's all. She's fun. You don't have to worry—I'm not going to ask her to go to the prom with me." He wiped his greasy fingers on a napkin and tossed it in the trash. "Besides, it's obvious she's crazy about you."

A tremor ran through me. Had Gio's emotional radar really improved this much?

"She is not," I said. "We're just friends."

"*Please.* I saw the way she looked at you—or rather, I *recognized* the way she looked at you."

We both stared at our shoes for a minute, and I wondered if Gio had the same lump in his throat that I had in mine. After a minute he shook his head. "I don't get it, Marisol. How come you're so crazy about Olivia when somebody like Lee is standing right in front of you?"

I cleared my throat. "Since when are you qualified to give advice on interpersonal relations?"

He smiled sheepishly and jammed his hands into his pockets. "I admit my track record is spotty, but I'm not blind. I can tell the real thing when I see it."

"And you don't think Olivia is the 'real thing'?" I said, sarcastically.

He looked off down the road, and I thought he was going to ignore my question, but finally he turned around and answered. "There's something wrong with her. Olivia. I mean, I know she's smart and sexy and everything, but something isn't right. I don't know—I just don't *trust* her."

It was on the tip of my tongue to snap back a nasty reply about his thin skin. Just because she hadn't liked his piece last week didn't mean there was something *wrong* with her. But then I didn't. Not because I agreed with him that Olivia was less than perfect, but because I knew he wasn't saying it out of spite. Even though Gio had told me some stupid lies when we first met, about his name and certain prom details, he had never told me an emotional lie. He was always truthful with me about his feelings—even when I didn't want him to be—which was a gift you didn't get from too many people. I'd asked Gio to be honest with me, so I shouldn't complain just because I didn't like what he had to say.

"Well, *I* trust her," I said, in a flattened voice that barely convinced me, much less Gio. "And I know her better than you do."

"Okay. You're right," he said, nodding. "I shouldn't have said anything. You like Olivia and she likes you. So that's great. What do I know?" He put his hand on my shoulder to convince me of his goodwill. "I'm sorry."

What *did* he know? Damn it, now I felt that little worm of doubt wriggling around in my brain, questioning the things I thought I believed. How on earth did you ever decide you loved and trusted one person more than another? It was obviously a leap of faith, and I was not normally the kind of person to leap without looking pretty damn closely at what I was leaping into.

After lunch we continued on down the Cape to Truro to pick up Diana so she could ride into P'town with us. She was waiting outside her house when we drove up, horsing around with a big brown mutt. The house looked pretty ramshackle, unpainted gray shingles, with gutters hanging off the sides and a crack in the front window.

I waved to Diana and then busied myself with extricating my feet from the jungle of books, water bottles, and coffee and doughnut trash that had grown up around them in just a few hours. I didn't want to actually *watch* Gio greeting Diana, but I did want to know how he did it, so I kept my cat-eyed lids low, observing slyly.

They both seemed to hesitate slightly as they came

together, but once there each sprang at the other, Diana throwing her arms around Gio's neck. A substantial kiss announced that their relationship had definitely progressed past friendship. Wow, okay, that was terrific. That was what I'd been hoping for. So, why did I suddenly feel kicked in the stomach the way you do when you realize the person you love no longer feels the same way about you? I never wanted anything to happen between Gio and me—nothing *could* happen. Was I so selfish that I didn't want anyone else to have him either? *Nice, Marisol. What a great friend you are.*

Gio introduced Diana to Lee, Birdie, and Damon, and then Diana gave me a brief hug, the kind you give to people you're a little scared of. I was pretty sure she hadn't been intimidated by me last spring—this had to do with Gio, and her fear that he still liked me. Liked me more than he should. I really tried not to feel good about that, and I almost succeeded.

Back in the car. Another ten minutes and we were at the condo in Provincetown, which more than lived up to its billing.

"Oh, my God," Diana said, staring out the second-floor picture window. "Look at this view! This is a million-dollar apartment!"

"That's exactly what it is," Birdie said proudly. "And we're getting it free for the weekend because the guys who own it *adore* my mother."

I checked out the bedrooms quickly and was relieved to find there were three of them—one each for me and Lee. That would make things much less awkward at bedtime. I put my bag in one of the two smaller rooms, knowing Birdie would squawk if he and Damon didn't get the master suite.

Lee stood at the picture window staring at the beach and the bay, which spread out below us. Finally she whispered, "Is that the ocean?"

"That's the bay," I said, "but it joins the ocean at Herring Cove Beach, not far from here. We'll go there to see the dunes. You will *love* the dunes!"

"And then we'll come back and sip champagne in the hot tub!" Birdie said as he pulled a big green bottle from his duffel bag.

"You brought champagne?" Gio said. "Jesus, it's a good thing we didn't get stopped."

"Oh, don't wet your knickers, Gramma," Birdie said. "I'm finally in Provincetown, and I'm celebrating!"

"Where are we going for dinner?" Damon wanted to know.

"You're thinking about dinner already?" I said. "We just had an enormous lunch an hour ago."

"Diana and I will go to the dunes with you, if that's okay, but we're having dinner at her house, with her dad," Gio said.

"But then we're coming back into town later to go dancing," Diana said, taking Gio's hand. "For old times' sake."

Gio blushed. "Yeah. Lousy dancer that I am."

"You aren't!" Diane said. "You're great!"

Oh, God, this could be weird. "So, you're going to Butterfield's, I guess," I said.

Diana nodded. "You guys should meet us there. You remember how much fun it is, Marisol."

What I remembered was dancing with June and B. J. and several other lesbians so I wouldn't ever be free to dance with Gio. I'd danced with him once, at his prom, and things had gotten totally out of control—I didn't intend to let that happen again. The trip to Provincetown was meant to show him that it wouldn't. Gio had danced with Diana that evening, which had probably given her the idea that eventually led to this weekend, her hand gripped firmly in his.

"Dancing! Absolutely!" Birdie said. "We intend to dance until we fall on our asses, don't we, Damon?"

But Damon had already fallen on his ass and was fast asleep in a lounge chair on the terrace.

CHAPTER TWENTY

SINCE THE AFTERNOON HAD GOTTEN quite warm, we put on our swimming suits and sandals and brought towels and warmer clothes with us to Herring Cove. The water was cold, but we all went in—even Damon—daring each other to go deeper and deeper until we were in over our heads. It was so calm I floated on my back, feeling more relaxed than I had in ages.

By the time we got out, the sun had gone behind clouds. Freezing, we hurriedly dried off and pulled sweatshirts and jeans on over our damp suits. Lee's teeth were actually chattering, and at first we gave her some grief about being a wimpy midwesterner. But when we saw that she really couldn't get warm, Gio and I made a sandwich with her in the middle and hugged her until her lips weren't blue anymore.

Okay, the three-way hug was a little weird, but it happened so spontaneously it didn't freak anybody out. It wasn't as if Gio and I were hugging each other—and yet I did feel as if all three of us were warming each other up. And I don't mean that in a sexual way. It was as if he and I were transmitting messages back and forth that said, *I like you a lot, you big idiot; we're still friends.* And Lee, in the middle, was not a buffer between us, but a conduit for the message, some of which was sticking to her, too.

When our huddle broke apart, Gio went right to Diana and gave her a big squeeze—to reassure her, I guess. As we trudged up the sand hill and into the dunes, Diana and Gio smooching on one side and Birdie and Damon bumping hips on the other, I suddenly realized that Lee and I were in the company of two couples. Lord, it's so uncomfortable to be the ones not in a relationship when everyone around you is making affectionate noises in pairs. Fortunately, Lee was falling in love with the landscape and didn't seem to notice the high hormone levels surrounding us.

After our hike Gio and Diana dropped us at the condo and went back to Truro. We cracked open Birdie's champagne and sat in the hot tub and then the lounge chairs, snoozing and getting slightly sloshed as the sun went down.

By eight o'clock we were showered and back out on the magical streets of Provincetown, threading our way through the throngs of gorgeous bodies, all tanned and muscled and homosexual. Every now and then we saw a heterosexual couple holding hands or pushing a stroller, but they were only tourists; the town didn't really belong to them the way it did to us. It was a feeling I'd never had anywhere else—that the world was really *mine*.

Birdie and Damon were indulging in their great mutual interest: shopping. They perused both the windows full of art objects and the men who passed by in tight pants and unbuttoned shirts—art objects themselves.

"Oh, my God," Birdie said, throwing his head back.

"Did you *see* him? He looked right at me!"

"He was looking at me," Damon said with certainty.

"I don't *think* so!" Birdie said, hands on his hips.

It gave them something to argue about until we got to Bubala's, the restaurant where I'd gotten us reservations.

"Can we eat outside? Please?" Birdie begged the hunky guy at the desk. We were escorted to a table near the sidewalk, where we could watch the singer across the street, dressed in drag and belting out torch songs, accompanying himself on a portable keyboard. The food was so good Lee and I could ignore the boys' heated discussion about what kind of wig looked best on a tall man with a five o'clock shadow.

"I never imagined there was any place like this," Lee said. "With the ocean and the dunes and the art galleries and all these *gay* people! This is heaven on earth."

"I know," I said, nodding. "That's why I wanted you to see it. There are a lot of us, Lee, and we know how to have fun!"

The dinner was great, and I even managed to talk Lee into sharing some tiramisu with me afterwards. Since Birdie was watching both his own weight and Damon's, they left before dessert arrived to go look at some paper lamps in a nearby shop.

Once we were alone, I found myself stealing little glances at Lee while she was eating. She looked so relaxed, and happier than I'd ever seen her. Her face was glowing from the afternoon sun, and when she looked up and saw me watching her, her slightly embarrassed smile was adorable.

"You've been so great to me, Marisol. I know I keep

thanking you and it sounds dumb, but I really mean it."

"Come on, Lee. You don't need to—"

"I know I don't, but I want to. I *have* to." She put her hand on my leg under the table—it was just a light touch, but it seemed electrified. "You probably know that I have kind of a crush on you. I guess it's because I'm so new at this, but I can't quite read your signals. Last night, at your parents' house, I brought up Olivia because I was hoping you'd tip your hand a little, but you didn't. I mean, are you really *with* her or what? You told your mother it was not a big deal, so I thought maybe . . . I don't know, I think you like me, but maybe you just want to be friends. Anyway, I wanted to tell you, if you were open to more than that . . ." She let the sentence hang in the air.

I was afraid to look into her eyes, and if we'd been alone, I don't think I would have dared. But at the noisy restaurant, with Birdie and Damon across the street, and tragic falsetto tunes being belted out a few yards away, it seemed safe.

Wrong. What I saw in her eyes was the same thing I'd seen in Gio's eyes the night of the prom last spring. Hope. Sadness. Love.

When Gio had told me he loved me, I'd gotten mad at him. He knew I was a lesbian, knew it was never going to happen that way for us. And he'd pushed it anyway. I'd seen it as male arrogance or heterosexual balls, that he thought I could be straight, would *want* to be straight, for him. But now that I'd announced my emotions to Olivia, I realized how hard it could be to hold back those words when they were ready to come out. Why shouldn't Lee hope that our friendship might become more than that? It might even have happened, if I hadn't met Olivia.

I was determined not to hurt Lee, not to ruin our friendship the way I'd almost ruined it with Gio. I squeezed her hand and scooted my chair closer to hers.

"Thank you," I said. "You're already a great friend, Lee, and I hope you always will be. But the thing is, I *am* still seeing Olivia, and it's pretty serious."

A veil fell over her eyes. "It is? You never talk about her."

I tightened my grip on her hand. "Well, I didn't want to hurt your feelings."

Lee looked into her lap. "You knew how I felt?"

"Lee, I'm flattered," I said. "And you know I like you. Hell, I wouldn't have asked you to come on this weekend if I didn't like you a lot!"

She nodded. "I know. It's fine. I just kept telling myself that if you were bringing me to Provincetown and not her . . ."

"Maybe, if I hadn't met Olivia . . ." I said, hoping she would fill in the blank. Instead, she just looked into my eyes, a penetrating look, as if she were searching for all my deep-down secrets.

And then, I don't know quite how it happened, all of a sudden I leaned in and kissed her. At the moment it seemed like the most natural thing in the world. Inevitable. And she kissed me back, and for about thirty seconds I totally forgot what I was doing.

Eventually panic arrived, but it was just a little late. I broke off the kiss and sat back in my chair, my heart thumping.

"Whoa," I said. "That was . . . I shouldn't have . . ."

"No, I know," Lee said, picking nervously at her bangs. "It was my fault anyway."

"It wasn't anybody's *fault*," I said, waving away her apology. "I mean, hey, what's a kiss between friends? No big deal, right?" I licked my lips and found that the taste of her still lingered there.

"Right." Lee smiled weakly but didn't look at me. She pointed to the chocolate-coated dessert that stood between us. "You haven't eaten any tiramisu," she said. "Don't make me eat it all."

I picked up my fork but barely knew what to do with it.

"Olivia must be great not to mind you coming down here without her," Lee said, as she chased a blob of cream around her plate.

I try so hard to be truthful with people. I used to think it was easy—I took pride in my policy of honesty-at-any-price. But the older I get, the more it seems like telling the truth isn't always such a straightforward business. Sometimes it's hard to know exactly what the truth *is*. And sometimes it takes a lot of explanation to get at the actual truth. True is not always the exact opposite of false.

"She probably *would* mind if she knew you were here," I said, finally. "She wasn't happy that I was going at all, so I didn't fill her in on all the details."

This news perked Lee up a little bit. "Oh. Would she be jealous if she knew I was here?"

Would she? Was she jealous when she thought I was going with Gio? Or was she just angry at my disloyalty?

"She'd be hurt that I didn't tell her," I said, ducking the question.

Just thinking of her seemed to bring Olivia's ghost to the table. I could feel her watching me, taking in the situation. Had I lied to her? Sort of. But hadn't it been necessary? What if she hadn't understood the truth? She certainly wouldn't have understood why I'd kissed Lee. I hated thinking about how angry Olivia would be if she knew that, but, like it or not, the thought of her had invaded my heart. Which made the tiramisu taste a little bit off.

Thank God Birdie hadn't seen the kiss. At least I'd be spared his pronouncements on my shameless behavior. Why had I kissed Lee? You don't kiss someone when you're trying to convince them that you're serious about someone else! It was the way she'd looked at me, so seriously, as if I meant so much to her. I couldn't resist.

But when you're in love with someone else, you *have* to resist. For God's sake, I'd hardly kissed anybody before this week, but now that the switch had been flipped, I was apparently willing to kiss everybody! No, that wasn't fair either—there *was* something between me and Lee, but it was something I couldn't let myself dwell on. I had a girlfriend; I didn't need another one. It wasn't fair to Olivia *or* Lee.

When we walked into Butterfield's at ten thirty, the place was just starting to fill up. Diana had told us that things didn't really get going until around eleven at the dance bars. She and Gio showed up about fifteen minutes after we did, and we managed to commandeer a table right on the edge of the dance floor, where we could watch the action.

Birdie and Damon started dancing immediately, both of them big show-offs with limited abilities—the kind of dancers you try not to get too close to for fear of being whacked in the head by a far-flung arm. Gio and Diana danced too, more sedately but not without their own sexiness, while Lee and I held down the table and watched the choreography in an uncomfortable silence. Gio and Diana came back first, breathing heavily.

"You two should dance now," Diana said. "We'll guard the table."

"I'm not much of a dancer," Lee said.

"That's what I said the first time I came here too," Gio told her. "Nobody cares what you look like. It's just fun."

She looked nervously at the dance floor, now filled with sweaty bodies gyrating to "I Love the Nightlife."

It was Lee's hesitance, that shy puppy quality, that I found attractive. Oddly, she was the exact opposite of Olivia in that respect. I really wanted to dance with Lee—what harm was there in a little booty-shaking, anyway? Maybe it would help us get past the weirdness of the kiss.

"What kind of music is this?" Lee wanted to know.

"Disco," I said. "And this is one of the last places on earth it hasn't been outlawed." I stood up and put out my hand. "Come on."

"Why don't you dance with Gio?" she said. "I'll watch."

"We'll all three dance together," Gio said, hauling Lee from her seat. "That way I won't look so boringly heterosexual."

I turned to check on Diana to see if this was okay with her and was happy to see that she seemed fine with the idea—

obviously this weekend was making her feel more secure about her relationship with Gio. I took Lee's other hand and we pulled her out onto the floor.

Gio and I jumped into the music, each of us holding one of Lee's hands. But it only took her a minute to fling us off and start to dance on her own. She was a perfectly good dancer, although a little embarrassed at first. But as the music pounded into our hearts, all three of us threw off our inhibitions and boogied like crazy. We danced from the edge of the crowd into the middle and out on the other side, our arms waving in the air. Lee's smile looked genuine again, which was a big relief—she seemed to have absorbed both my rebuff and the confusing kiss without too much damage. Just as the song was reaching its fevered conclusion, my eyes swept the crowd at the edge of the dance floor with a challenging look, as if I were saying, *I'm shaking my butt in front of the whole world, and you, chicken shit, are just standing there like a telephone pole.* Because, after all, dancing is 90 percent attitude, right?

But something caught my eye, stopped my gaze from roaming, and held it steady. There was a woman staring at me as I whirled in circles, an *enraged* woman, and she was no ghost. I turned back to look at her again. Yes, indeed, it was Olivia.

Jesus Christ, what was she doing here? As soon as she knew I'd seen her, she turned and plowed back through the crowd toward the door. I stopped dancing so fast I almost fell over.

"Wait! Olivia!" I yelled as I took off after her, but the music was just segueing into an eardrum-bursting version of "If I Can't Have You," and everybody started singing along.

It was a good thing Olivia was wearing a red blouse, because it helped me catch glimpses of her as she stalked off. Once we were outside, I yelled to her.

"Olivia! Stop! Let me talk to you!"

She pulled herself up in the middle of the alley and turned to wait for me to catch up to her. I don't know when I've ever seen anybody look that angry.

"I didn't know you were thinking of coming down here," I said.

"That's obvious. I wasn't 'thinking' of it, until I noticed that both you *and* your boyfriend skipped my class this morning. Imagine my surprise to find you both here together, sweating to the oldies." She spit out the final words: "You lied to me, Marisol."

"I didn't!"

She leaned into my face and hissed, "There is nothing I despise more than a woman who pretends to be a lesbian, but then the minute a man shows up, she's suddenly straight as a ruler."

"That's not what happened. I'm not like that! I was planning to come with Birdie and Damon, and Gio was going to visit his girlfriend in Truro. It was a coincidence. When we realized we were all coming here the same weekend, we decided to drive down together, that's all."

She stared hard into my eyes, trying to decide whether or not to believe me. "Isn't that cozy?" she said finally, her voice low and thick as tar.

"It's the truth." My eyes were doing their best Labrador retriever impression, begging for forgiveness.

"And where are Birdie and Damon now?"

"They're inside, dancing. Come on, I'll show you."

She didn't budge. "You better be telling me the truth, Marisol."

"I am!"

The fury drained away from her, but it left behind a residue of suspicion. "You should have told me," she said.

"I know," I said, chewing on my cheek. "I'm sorry."

"So, is that Gio's girlfriend?" she said, motioning back toward Butterfield's. "The one who was flailing around with the two of you on the dance floor?"

"Um, the girl we were dancing with?" I said, stalling for time. It was immediately clear to me that I would have to lie or face further fury. Olivia had met Diana at the arts fair a few weeks ago, but obviously she hadn't paid much attention to her. So, the question was not whether to lie, but whether I could get away with the lie. How the mighty had fallen.

"Yeah, yes, that's her," I said, becoming the liar I had just begged Olivia to believe I was not.

She shook her head. "I thought you were coming down here with two gay guys, Marisol. Not an entire gay-straight alliance."

"They're just my friends, Olivia. Don't be mad at me."

"How am I supposed to trust you, after this?"

"After *what*? I haven't done anything!"

"You've let me down. You've hurt my feelings. You aren't the person I thought you were."

Tears started to gush from my eyes when she said that, maybe because I wasn't the person *I* thought I was either. "I never meant to hurt your feelings. Please, Olivia! I'm so sorry!"

I was bawling like a damn baby by the time Olivia finally relented and put her arms around me. "Okay," she said. "I guess I'll give you a second chance. You should know, though, I seldom give anyone the opportunity to hurt me twice. Consider yourself fortunate."

"I won't hurt you again. I promise!" I sobbed.

"Once you said you'd *never* hurt me," she reminded me, giving me a kiss on the forehead. "I'm going back to my guest house now—this whole day has just exhausted me. I'll pick you up at ten o'clock tomorrow morning. Where are you staying?"

"The Bull Ring Condominiums. On Commercial at Pearl Street. Apartment Two."

"Fine. We'll have breakfast, and then you can ride back to the city with me."

I almost protested. After all, I'd invited Lee to come on the trip with me, and, especially after everything that had happened, it wasn't very nice of me to leave her alone with the guys. Besides, I wanted another whole day in Provincetown with everybody. We'd talked about going swimming at Race Point.

But how could I say no to Olivia after this? I couldn't explain without telling her who Lee really was, and she would never trust me if she knew I'd lied to her *again*. And it wasn't as if spending Sunday with Olivia was really a sacrifice—as long as she wasn't still mad at me. Fortunately, the guys all liked Lee, especially Gio. I figured she'd be fine with them.

As I straightened up and looked at Olivia, I noticed Gio and Lee lurking outside the door to Butterfield's, checking on me, I guess. God, had they witnessed this entire spectacle?

"Okay," I said to Olivia, brushing away a few last tears. "I'll see you tomorrow morning then."

"You still love me, don't you?" she said, loud enough for my friends to hear.

She cocked her head sideways and smiled, but the words rang in my ears. Why was she reminding me of my declaration before she'd said the words back to me? I nodded mutely.

Olivia leaned in and kissed me again, this time on the lips, long and hard. Even while I was enjoying it, it occurred to me that Olivia had seen Gio and Lee standing in the shadows too, and this show was for them.

CHAPTER TWENTY-ONE

WHAT DO YOU MEAN you're leaving in the morning?" Birdie said. "You can't just desert us like that!"

We were on our way back to the condo, the early fall breezes chilly after the heat of the bar.

"I'm not deserting you. I'm just leaving early," I said. "Olivia is a little upset, and—"

"Well, so am I! Why do you have to do what she wants?" Birdie said. "We had plans for tomorrow, and she's wrecking everything. I'm changing my mind about Olivia; she's too bossy. You need a nice, normal girl, like Lee."

"Shut up, Birdie!" I gave him the evilest eye possible. Did he have to give voice to every thought that passed through his hyperactive brain? No wonder he and my mother got along so well—neither of them could leave a thought unspoken. Lee was being very quiet, barely looking up from the pavement as we walked six abreast down the now-deserted street.

"I'm not crazy about Olivia either," Gio chimed in. "I mean, she's not a bad teacher, but there's something so smug about her. Sort of arrogant."

"Arrogant!" Birdie echoed. "That's the word I was trying to think of!"

"You've only gone out with her a few times," Gio said. "You aren't *engaged* to her. I don't see why she had to follow you down here and mess up your weekend."

"She isn't arrogant," I mumbled. I didn't intend to have a big conversation about this. I just wanted to get off the subject, but apparently that would not be possible.

"You don't like her either?" Birdie asked Gio. "Man, I never thought I'd have anything in common with *you*!"

"Yeah, you're practically twins now," I said. "Could everybody please stop bashing my girlfriend?"

Damon cleared his throat. "Maybe Olivia just feels a little insecure about your relationship. Everybody feels that way sometimes."

Birdie put his arm around the big lug's waist. "But not you, amigo! Because I am loyal as a puppy!"

"Yeah, except when you're calling me an idiot, or a pig, or something."

"Damon, I adore idiots and pigs!"

"I'm sorry," Gio said. "I'm just disappointed. We had so much fun today; I hate that you have to leave early tomorrow."

"Well, I'm sorry to leave early too, but sometimes you have to accommodate your partner, you know?" As soon as I said it, I knew "partner" was not the right word to describe Olivia. A partner was someone with whom you were on equal footing, which did not seem to apply to the two of us, at least not at the moment. After that scene outside Butterfield's I felt more like the princess's naughty child. The brilliant and beautiful princess's naughty child, but still. I buried my hands in my back pockets and my own disappointment deep inside.

"Olivia is gorgeous," Damon said, sincerely.

Birdie laughed. "We're not blind, honey!"

But I appreciated my newest roommate's plainspoken assessment of the situation. Olivia *was* gorgeous, and I was lucky to be with her. Even if she wasn't in love with me, she was sleeping with me, so she must like me pretty damn much—what was I moping around for? I thanked Damon silently and let him advance a few rungs up the ladder of my affection.

Before Gio and Diana veered off to the parking lot at the wharf, the five of them made their plans for the next day, including an afternoon trip to Race Point before heading back to the city. I tried not to care that I wouldn't be joining them, this motley crew who wouldn't even know each other if it weren't for me.

Diana gave me a hug. "I guess I won't see you tomorrow. Have fun with Olivia." I had the feeling Diana knew exactly what was going on in my head, in everybody's head, and she forgave us all for our mistakes even before we made them. Lucky Gio, to be with her.

Lee hadn't said a word to me since the incident with Olivia at the bar, and I wondered what was going on in her head. We were all tired by the time we got back to the condo and went to our own rooms. But I knew I wouldn't be able to sleep if I didn't say something to her that night—in the morning I'd be too rushed. So I put on my bathrobe and knocked on her closed door.

"Come in." She was sitting up in bed, wearing just the kind of Indiana-girl flannel pajamas I would have expected her to wear, writing in a book.

"Hey," I said. "Is that your journal?"

She nodded and closed it. "I like to write things down before I forget how I feel."

I tried for a rueful laugh. "So, I suppose tonight's entry memorializes me for posterity as a selfish jerk, huh?"

Her smile was icy. "Get over yourself, Marisol."

Worse than I thought. "Listen, Lee, I feel really bad leaving you here with people you don't know very well, but you seem to get along fine with the guys. I can tell you like Gio, right? So, it's not *that* terrible if I leave early, is it?"

"Why are you even asking me? You'll do what you want to do, no matter what I say." She wouldn't even look at me.

I sighed and sank into a chair in the corner. "You're really mad at me."

"Not about that. I get along fine with the others, and I do like Gio. I think we're a lot alike."

"Yeah, I can see that," I said. Which is when it occurred to me that I'd once abandoned Gio down here too, when I left the zine conference early with June and her friends from New York. But that time I'd felt I had to escape; this time I felt almost as if I were being dragged away. Which was ridiculous: I was leaving with Olivia, who I was crazy about.

"I'm just plain old jealous, if you want to know the truth," Lee said, finally meeting my eyes. "Which I'm sure you don't. You've got a beautiful girlfriend who I could never compete with. You didn't even bother to tell me it was your brilliant writing teacher you were dating—Gio told me that. Anyway, I'm mostly mad at myself for thinking there could ever be something between us. But don't worry, I'll get over it." She brought her flannel-covered knees up to her chest and hugged them.

I didn't know what to say. She and Gio had more in common than she knew—maybe they'd bond over it on the ride home.

Finally I said, "You know I really like you, Lee. A lot. It might have happened between us if I hadn't met Olivia."

"Yeah, you mentioned that."

"Lee, you're a great person. You'll find a girlfriend—I'm sure of it."

"You think that's the answer, don't you? Just get Lee a girlfriend. Any old girlfriend. You really don't get it, do you?"

I got it; I just didn't *want* to get it. "I'm sorry. How about if we get together this week back in town? Maybe we can go to a movie or something? At the Brattle, if you want. Are they still showing those Tennessee Williams films?"

She was quiet for a minute. "I think I need a little time to myself this week."

I tried to ignore the solemnity in her voice.

"Come on, we can still be friends, can't we?"

She looked at me sadly. "I want to be part of your life, Marisol. I just need to figure out how to do it without feeling like shit. Do you understand that?"

Congratulations, Marisol. You've hurt yet another person you really care about.

"Will you call me when you're ready to see me again?"

She nodded.

"Okay. Well, good night then."

"Good night."

We all overslept the next morning, but Lee was gracious enough to give me the first shower in the bathroom we shared. I was stuffing my clothes into my backpack when Olivia showed up. Jesus, why didn't I think these things through ahead of time? If I'd been ready earlier, I could have waited outside; now, not only would Birdie get to put in his unpredictable two cents' worth, but what if Olivia saw Lee—who I'd told her was Gio's girlfriend—in the condo? How could I explain that?

Olivia stepped through the door in white shorts and a black halter top, which left a great deal of skin exposed to the morning sun. Those long, tan legs were unbelievable, and I started thinking about how, when we got back to Boston, maybe we'd go to her apartment again. Yeah, this day might turn out to be incredible, as long as it wasn't sabotaged in the next ten minutes.

"Nice place," Olivia said. "How'd you get it?"

"Birdie's mother is a realtor," I said.

She shook her head. "Say no more. You rich kids love living off the largesse of Mommy and Daddy, don't you?"

She gave a little laugh as she said it, and I assumed she meant the remark as a joke, but Birdie, just entering the kitchen, didn't see the humor.

He pulled a bowl from the cupboard and banged it onto the countertop so hard I thought it would break. "Who made you Judge Judy?"

"Birdie's inner comedian isn't awake yet," I said.

He mumbled something, and I didn't ask him to repeat it.

"So, we have to get going, right?" I asked Olivia.

"That would be my preference," she said.

"Okay, I just have to stick my bathroom stuff into my bag and I'm good to go."

Even though I ran through the bathroom like Jackie Joyner-Kersee, as I was returning to the kitchen I heard Olivia say, "Oh, hi, you're John's girlfriend, aren't you?" And sure enough, there stood Lee, blindsided by her nemesis before she'd even had breakfast. Now the truth would come out and I would be tarred and feathered, rightly, by both of them.

Fortunately, Olivia didn't wait for an answer to her question, but forged ahead. "I'm Marisol's friend, Olivia. I didn't think you and John were staying here. Marisol said you lived in Truro."

Damon walked into the room just then and swapped greetings with Olivia, which gave Lee a minute to figure out what assumptions Olivia was making about her. She settled back on her heels and looked Olivia right in the eyes. "Oh, I do live in Truro. We didn't stay here; we just arrived before these sleepyheads were out of the shower."

Damon looked back and forth between the two of them, completely in the dark, an unexploded grenade that could blow me up at any second.

"Complete sloths, aren't they?" Olivia agreed. "Where is John anyway?"

"He ran out to get us some bacon and eggs for breakfast," Lee said, the story slipping smoothly off her tongue. "These guys didn't bring much to eat."

I was clutching the back of a kitchen chair so hard my fingers were cramping. Lee was a saint to lie for me like this; I owed her, big time. I watched as Birdie took a box of cereal out of the bag of food we'd brought with us. Lee's lie must have reverberated in his head until it made sense, because after half a minute he dropped the box back into the bag.

"Oh, he's getting eggs? I didn't know that. Good, I like eggs," he mumbled.

"Little early in the morning for you, Jughead?" Olivia said, smiling.

"Okay, we're out of here," I said, before Birdie could think of a rejoinder. I turned to Lee. "Tell Gio I said goodbye and thanks for the ride down." When I hugged her, she stiffened under my fingers and barely hugged me back. I tried to transmit my thank-yous and I'm-sorrys psychically, hoping she'd be able to read my mind.

As I squeezed past Damon, praying he was still too stupefied to speak, he grabbed me in an awkward embrace. "Bye, Marisol," he said. "If Gio doesn't come back soon, *Diana* and I will go out looking for him. We need eggs!" He was so proud of himself for figuring out the conundrum and fitting himself sideways into the deceitful little play, I gave him a hearty pat on the back.

By the time I got into Olivia's car, there was sweat dripping down the sides of my face. And the morning was not that warm.

"I say we get on the road and stop for breakfast up in Wellfleet," Olivia suggested. She obviously wanted to put distance between me and Provincetown as soon as possible. I agreed, but turned around to watch my favorite place on earth disappear behind me in the rear window, like in some cheesy movie where the kid is forcibly removed from home and sits in the backseat tearfully giving it one last look.

Once we hit Wellfleet, Olivia softened considerably. All the tension seemed to leave her, and she became the charming person who'd enchanted me the first time I met her. She fed me bites of her omelet to go with my French toast, and she scooped a drip of syrup off my chin with her finger, then put the finger in my mouth. She ordered us cocoa with marshmallows and licked the foam off my lips. And I was sad about trading this for an afternoon at the beach? Was I nuts?

On the drive home she started to tell me about trips she wanted to take sometime, not just to Cape Cod, but to San Francisco, Europe, Brazil. She didn't seem to have traveled much, but she'd read about lots of places, and she described them to me in detail.

"Maybe you'd like to come with me?" she said.

"That would be great," I said. I could imagine it—the two of us discovering the world together.

"We'll see, won't we?" she said, teasing. "If I can trust you."

My stomach clenched. I hated that I'd lied to Olivia rather than explain my friendship with Lee. I hadn't wanted her to get mad at me; her anger was so transforming. But what now? If Olivia and I kept dating, there would surely come a time when we'd bump into Lee, or maybe Gio and Diana. I couldn't ask everyone I knew to keep on lying for me. Gio had once called me a "truth zealot," but lately I'd proved him wrong about that. Lying so you didn't hurt some-one's feelings was one thing, but lying out of fear was another, and it made me very uncomfortable. I'd never tolerated lying in other people; how could I accept it in myself?

The farther away from Provincetown we got, the better Olivia's mood became. Once we were on Route 3 headed for Boston, she stepped on the gas and sang along with a Bonnie Raitt song on the radio.

"So, do you want to know what your class assignment is for next week?" she asked.

"Sure."

"Not hard. I want you to find five outstanding first lines from novels and tell me why they make you want to read the whole book. And then I want you to write the first line of your own novel." She smiled at me. "Since you already have a first line, you're ahead of the game."

"Oh, that'll be fun!"

"I thought so."

"What's the first line of your novel?" I asked.

"What?" She looked startled.

"Your novel. The one you're finishing up."

"Marisol, you know I don't like anyone to know anything about my work until it's completely finished."

"Not even the first line? You can't even tell me *that*?" I said, laughing.

"No, I can't!" Her bite was back, and it was just as bad as her bark. I turned away from her and looked out the side window. Once again I felt we weren't on equal footing. I was the kid, and she was the grown-up who could put me in my place at any moment. Which totally sucked.

Olivia reached over and patted my knee. "I'm sorry. I don't mean to be secretive. You know, anxiety is the hand-maiden of creativity."

God, she had a saying for every occasion. "What are you anxious about?"

"I'm very near to finishing the book, Marisol. As a mat-ter of fact, I may be able to finish it this week."

"Really? And then can I read it?"

She sighed. "You are so persistent! *Eventually*, you can read it, yes."

I had another idea. "Maybe I could read some of your stories! The ones you had published in those magazines!"

"Oh, I don't have those in my apartment. I sent them to my parents for safekeeping."

"You don't have the files on your computer anymore?"

She shook her head. "Deleted them. You don't need them if you have the magazines."

"Well, what are the names of the magazines?"

Olivia threw her head back in apparent frustration. "Marisol, just let it go, would you?"

I was beginning to think she didn't want me to read any of her stuff, which hurt my feelings. Did she think I was too young to understand it, or what?

Olivia had started talking about herself and didn't notice my annoyance.

"I love being so close to the end of the story. Endings are so magical," she said. "If the doctor told me I had six minutes to live, I'd just type a little faster. When I stop working, the rest of the day is posthumous. I'm only really alive when I'm writing."

"Not when you're having sex?" I said it in a snotty tone of voice, but Olivia just laughed.

"Well, that wakes me up too," she said. "Are you hinting that you want to come over to my apartment when we get back?"

I shrugged. "If you want me to," I said, as if I hadn't started getting excited immediately.

"I think it's a great idea." Olivia arched her lovely neck and smiled at me. Then she said, "That girl Diana—I thought I'd met her once before, at the Arts Festival. But she looked different this morning."

My brain was momentarily paralyzed, and I could feel the lie cracking my heart in half. "She did? You only saw her for a minute."

"Yes, but I have a very good memory for faces."

I sat there frozen, unable to continue the lie or admit to it.

Finally she spoke again. "Well, I guess we all make mistakes, don't we?" she said.

I stared at her, my stomach churning, but nothing about her face, or her posture, or the way she clutched the wheel answered my question. Could she possibly *know*?

Chapter Twenty-Two

THAT AFTERNOON, IN HER BEDROOM, Olivia was definitely in charge. Which was fine. I mean, it was certainly exciting; Olivia knew what she was doing, and she had me completely in her control. The thing was, I didn't really like being controlled, being the passive one to whom things were done, no matter how pleasant those things were. Maybe I was being oversensitive because of the way the rest of the weekend had gone, but it seemed like another example of the ways in which we were not on even ground. Just because she was older, did that mean she would always be the commander in chief of our relationship? Taking a backseat wasn't really a facet of my personality.

Around four o'clock she rolled over and peered at the clock. "Time to jump in the shower. I'm meeting someone for drinks before dinner."

"You're going out *again*?"

"Yes. Do you have a problem with that?" She climbed out of bed and stood there, hands on her hips, perfectly naked, nakedly perfect.

"No, but, well, I thought maybe we could, I don't know . . ."

"You thought we could roll around in bed all day and all night? I have other things to do, Marisol!"

"That's not what I meant! I thought maybe the two of us could go out somewhere."

"Not tonight," she said curtly, throwing on a robe and heading into the bathroom. "I'm meeting someone important."

You didn't need to hit me in the head with a brick—clearly, *I* was not "someone important" to Olivia. And it was obvious that all but a very small portion of her life was being kept secret from me. Though she had no qualms about interfering with *my* plans, I wasn't supposed to know about hers. I wasn't invited to meet her friends or even know who they were. I couldn't read her novel or even hear the first sentence of it! What kind of a relationship was that?

I got up and dressed quickly, then went to her computer, this time with a purpose. As I'd hoped, it was turned on. The screensaver gave way to the same menu page as before. This time I scanned the short list of folders carefully.

```
Ideas for Stories
Lillian
Adult Ed Class Notes
Writing Quotes
Books I've Read
Books to Read
Miscellaneous
```

And that was all. An oddly brief list, I thought, for a writer. Did she delete everything the minute she finished it? And where was the actual manuscript for *Lillian, Who Says She Loves You*?

I went to the Lillian folder first, but there was no more in it than there had been the week before. Only notes, not an "almost finished" novel. I opened Ideas for Stories, which was exactly that. Half a dozen pages of ideas. Character sketches, a few chunks of dialogue, a description of an interesting setting. But no chapters.

Since some of the folders were clearly not relevant, I skipped down to Miscellaneous, but there wasn't much of interest there either: a bunch of saved articles from the *New York Times* and the *Boston Globe*, mostly about writers or books; an old itinerary from a trip to Bermuda in 2005; some information about how to exchange tickets at the American Repertory Theatre.

I went back to the menu page and clicked around from there, trying to find some file on this computer where Olivia's book might be saved. But there was nothing. I wondered if she knew I'd been looking at her computer, so she'd downloaded the novel onto a disc and hidden it somewhere. Would she really do that, just to keep me from reading a few pages? I opened desk drawers, looking for discs, but the only ones I found were still in their packaging and looked new. I was stumped. How far would she go to keep me from seeing her novel? Or was I being ridiculously paranoid?

Back to the menu page again. I clicked on Writing Quotes, just in case *Lillian* was buried under a heading meant to confuse me. A long document came up, one quotation after another, alphabetized by author. I gave up—the novel was not there either—and began to half-heartedly peruse the list. As I scanned, lines began to jump out at me. At first I didn't remember where I'd heard them before.

"Literature is the question minus the answer."
—*Roland Barthes*

"Writing a novel is like driving a car at night. You can only see as far as your headlights, but you can make the whole trip that way." —*E. L. Doctorow*

"Anxiety is the handmaiden of creativity."
—*T. S. Eliot*

That was the one that stopped me; I'd heard it only a few hours before, but I'd assumed it was just another one of Olivia's ingenious observations. And then it all fell into place. I looked at the list again.

"The worst enemy to creativity is self-doubt."
—*Sylvia Plath*

"The difference between the right word and the almost right word is the difference between lightning and a lightning bug." —*Mark Twain*

For God's sake, Olivia went around spouting these quotations as if she'd thought them all up herself! One after another! Weren't teachers supposed to be extra careful about stuff like that? Maybe it wasn't exactly plagiarism, but it sure smelled a lot like it. It was cheating, that I was sure of, to make your students think you could come up with smart, pithy sayings like these hour after hour. I was so stunned by this revelation that I didn't hear the shower go off. When I looked up, Olivia was standing a few feet away from me, smirking.

"Snooping, are we?" she said.

"Yeah, I guess I am," I said.

"Find what you were looking for?"

"No," I said. "But I found this." I turned the screen so she could see it.

Her face drew closed, and I could see she was furious. "Well, I hope you're satisfied. When you invade someone's privacy, you shouldn't be surprised to find something you don't really want to see."

As always, she'd confused me. Shouldn't I be angry with her? Shouldn't she be apologizing to me? Instead *she* was mad. Okay, I was snooping, but look what I'd found!

She walked to her closet and began yanking clothes off hangers and throwing them on. "You were trying to find my novel, weren't you? That's what you were looking for, isn't it?"

"I was," I admitted. "I don't understand why you won't let me see just a little of it. You read *my* writing."

"I'm your teacher!" she spat out. "It's my job."

"Is it also your job to make us think you came up with all these clever insights that are really the exact words of a bunch of famous writers?"

"What difference does it make?" she said, pulling a pair of hose up over a sculpted knee. "Those bozos wouldn't remember who said it even if I told them."

Bozos? "It makes a difference to me! You took the credit and I trusted you!"

She was quiet while she slipped her delicate feet into a pair of black heels; then she looked up at me and said, "And now you don't?"

"I—I don't know. I'm just shocked. I thought you hated lying as much as I did."

Olivia's voice got quiet. "And yet you lied to me, too, didn't you?" She disappeared back into the bathroom, leaving the arrow lodged in my heart. If I wasn't truthful with her, what right did I have to expect her to be truthful with me? When she came out again, she had on makeup and long, dangly earrings. She looked fantastic, and I wondered who would have the benefit of her dazzling company tonight.

"I told you I was sorry. I didn't think my lie was a big deal," I said. "It's not like Gio was going with me as my boyfriend. I was afraid you'd misunderstand."

"So you said. But if you've told me one lie, how do I know there aren't more?" She took a red leather jacket from her closet and slipped it on. "Anyway, we've each disappointed the other today, haven't we? Shall we just call it a draw and put the whole thing behind us?" Her mouth smiled, but I could tell her heart wasn't in it.

Having Olivia mad at me made me feel sick to my stomach, so I was relieved at whatever ragged reconciliation we could patch together. When I looked into her eyes, I still adored her. I still wanted to be with her. Even if she lied, even if I didn't understand her, I still wanted her to love me.

We didn't say much in the car, but Olivia kissed me before I got out, and I tried to convince myself everything was still okay between us. It had to be okay.

Birdie and Damon weren't home yet—they'd obviously made a day of it on the Cape—and I was pretty jumpy after the showdown with Olivia. I made myself coffee and a sandwich and took them into my room, thinking that doing the assignment for next week—such an easy, fun task—would get my mind off the day's events. I pulled a chair up to my bookshelf and read the beginnings of some of my favorite books. I hit gold on my first try.

Feed by M. T. Anderson was a book I'd picked up by chance at a used-book store, and as soon as I opened it, I remembered that I'd actually bought it because the first line was so great. "We went to the moon to have fun, but the moon turned out to completely suck." I laughed out loud in the bookstore and immediately read on. I had to know who this smartass kid was and what future he lived in where a trip to the moon was so commonplace he'd describe it as "sucking"—like a bad high-school dance. It was a hilarious line, and the rest of the book hadn't let me down either. So, that was number one on the list.

I was surprised to find that some of my favorite books did not start out with a bang, so I guess you don't necessarily *have* to hook your audience with the first line. But then again, when I did find a book with a dynamite first line, the rest of it was usually excellent too. So maybe if the first line is perfect, it sets the right tone for the author, too—I could see how that might work.

Anyway, these were the others I ended up with:

2. "It was the last day of our old lives, and we didn't even know it." Richard Peck wrote that in *Fair Weather*. I love a sentence like that; it's sad and exciting at the same time. You know there's going to be some nostalgia involved and somebody might even die before the book is over, but you also know there's a good story coming.

3. "Ships at a distance have every man's wish on board." This is from *Their Eyes Were Watching God* by Zora Neale Hurston. I might like this one a little better if it said "every man *and woman's* wish," or maybe just "everyone's wish," because that would keep the rhythm of the line intact. Still, it's a beautiful thought, and sad at the same time because the ships are "at a distance." But it's also funny, because if the ships came to shore, "every man" might actually have to get *on* one and not just wistfully wish for what he can't have. In other words, it's safe to wish you were out there sailing away, as long as you know it's not really possible.

4. "It was a queer, sultry summer, the summer they electrocuted the Rosenbergs, and I didn't know what I was doing in New York." That, of course, is Sylvia Plath from *The Bell Jar*. Yeah, she had a dark sensibility, but you have to love the way "sultry" puts the electricity in the air and *then* she brings in the Rosenbergs. You know right away New York is not going to be a hospitable climate for old Sylvia.

5. "I write this sitting in the kitchen sink." Dodie Smith, a British author, wrote that in a novel called *I Capture the Castle*. My mother gave me this book for my birthday last year, and I was skeptical because the cover looked very

old-fashioned and not like my kind of book at all. But again, that first sentence pulled me in. For one thing the narrator is writing, which is something I always appreciate in a character. But she's also sitting in a sink, and you want to know why. The author paints a picture of this weird, old, falling-down castle populated by a family of eccentrics; within a few pages you know that sitting in the sink is the least of their peculiarities.

Finding five good first lines was easier than I thought it would be. In fact I found a sixth one too, from one of my favorite childhood books, *The Voyage of the Dawn Treader*, which is part of the Narnia series by C. S. Lewis. The line is: "There was a boy called Eustace Clarence Scrubb, and he almost deserved it." Really makes you want to meet that kid, doesn't it?

I already had the first line of my novel written: *Christina had always believed she was born lucky—smart, funny, and just good-looking enough to get pretty much everything she wanted, except, of course, the thing she longed for most: love.* I sighed. Was I really going to make poor Christina follow in my own pathetic footsteps? Apparently, I was.

It was after seven o'clock by then, and I started wondering why Birdie and Damon weren't home yet. As I washed the dishes we'd left in the sink the morning before, I imagined them in the car, Lee up front with Gio, the other two in back. I knew Lee was angry with me for not telling her about Olivia, and I was hoping Gio would talk to her about it. If anybody knew what a jerk I could be sometimes, it was Gio. And he'd forgiven me, finally. So maybe Lee would too. *Hey, nobody's perfect, right?* Even, as I'd just realized, Olivia.

When the phone rang, I hoped it might be Olivia calling from the restaurant to say she wasn't really angry anymore. To make plans for later in the week. But no.

"Hey, it's Gio." He sounded weird, and I got a little scared for a minute.

"Hey, yourself. Where are you guys? You didn't have an accident or something, did you?"

"No. We're at the airport."

"The airport? Why?"

He sighed heavily. "We're here with Lee. She's really upset, Marisol. I thought you should know—she's determined to get a flight back to Indiana tonight. All she's got with her is the stuff she took to the Cape and her sister's credit card."

"What? You can't let her do that!"

"Don't make this *my* fault. After you left, she tried to be okay with it, but she's crazy about you, Marisol. I *told* you that. Birdie said there was a scene with Olivia this morning that Diana and I missed. It was downhill after that, and by the time we started driving back this afternoon, she admitted she was miserable. She said she needed to be someplace that felt like home, and that wasn't Cambridge or any place near you. As soon as we got to Boston, she begged me to take her right to the airport. What was I supposed to do?"

"Well, let me talk to her, then."

"She won't talk to you, Marisol. She doesn't even know I'm calling you. She's in the ticket line with Birdie and Damon. I said I was going to the bathroom so she wouldn't get suspicious."

"Shit." I banged my hand on the kitchen counter. "I guess I didn't handle this very well. It's my fault."

Gio didn't dispute me.

"Did she say how long she wants to stay in Indiana? She's planning to come back, isn't she?"

"I really don't know," Gio said. "I don't think *she* knows at the moment. She just wants to get away. You should understand that, Marisol. You're the great escape artist."

He didn't say it nastily, but I felt the sting anyway. "I didn't mean to hurt her, Gio. I like Lee. I like her a lot."

"You never *mean* to hurt anybody," Gio said. "They get hurt anyway." And, of course, he knew.

Chapter Twenty-Three

WHEN BIRDIE AND DAMON GOT BACK, I was sitting in the living room waiting for them. Birdie dropped his duffel bag just inside the front door. Damon picked it up and took it and his own bag into their room.

"Well, the weekend started out pretty good, but you missed the really fun part," Birdie said, dripping sarcasm.

"Just tell me, did she get a flight? Did she really leave?"

"What time is it?"

"Nine fifteen."

"Should have taken off about ten minutes ago. Mumsy and Pops will be picking her up around ten thirty p.m., allowing for the time change. You really did it this time, Marisol."

I let my mouth drop open. "Why is everybody blaming this on me? She knew I had another girlfriend." I couldn't tell them about the kiss—I could barely admit to myself that I'd given Lee a reason to hope and then thrown Olivia right in her face.

"Oh, is Olivia your girlfriend? I thought she was your keeper. What I want to know is why she had to follow you to the Cape. Lee felt totally humiliated by the whole thing, especially that stupid lie you told this morning about her being Gio's girlfriend."

"I didn't—I don't—" I stuttered, then gave up the defense. "I don't know why I do anything anymore. I like Lee; I never meant to hurt her feelings. And I didn't think she'd just *leave*."

"You knew what she was going through—she said you were the only person she could talk to about it. It's been a tough couple of months for her; she depended on you. And she totally fell for you, which you *knew*."

"Did she tell you that?"

Birdie nodded.

Damon came back into the room and sat on the couch. "It's a hard position to be in, Birdie. If someone is crazy about you and you don't feel the same way. What was Marisol supposed to do?"

Birdie thought about it before he answered. "If the person who's crushing on you is totally wrong for you, that's one thing—you just have to make them understand it right away and move on. But that wasn't the case here, was it? You liked Lee. She said you told her that if it hadn't been for Olivia, something might have happened between you."

"True, but Olivia *did* happen."

"But it could have happened with Lee," he persisted.

"Yes, I suppose so. I mean, at first I thought of Lee as kind of young and innocent and not terribly interesting. But as I got to know her better, I realized there was a lot more to her that you didn't see immediately."

"Yeah, with some people, it takes a while to see how great they are. Not everybody has that drop-dead thing going for them, like Olivia, where everybody on earth falls in love with them for at least five minutes."

"That's not how it is with me. I really love Olivia." *Most of the time.*

"Yeah, whatever," Birdie said, brushing off love like dandruff. "I'm saying, Olivia is not going to last."

"Oh, and how do you know that?"

Birdie stared at me hard, but it was Damon who put it into words. "Because she's Olivia," he said quietly.

"Whereas," Birdie continued, "Lee, if you'd given her half a chance, might not have been a crazy, whirlwind lovefest, but she would have lasted."

"And what makes you suddenly the big expert on love?" I asked, my throat tightening a bit.

Birdie looked at Damon, who smiled. "He took half a chance on me," Damon said. "And that worked out."

"Sweetheart, I don't do anything by halves," Birdie said, kissing Damon on the cheek. "Believe me, I threw my whole self, plus a couple of personalities I didn't even know I had, into capturing you. 'Cause you are my prince!"

Okay, gag me. Enough is enough.

I stood up. "I'm going to bed. I'll take your advice to the lovelorn under consideration, although I don't know what I can do about it now anyway. Lee's gone."

"Airplanes fly across the country both ways, hon," Birdie said.

***

Work that week was a huge suckage. The new part-timer Doug had hired to take some of Sophie's hours was a skinny middle-aged woman who slapped the sandwiches together any old way so she could save up enough seconds to stand in the back doorway letting in cold air and puffing on cigs every five minutes. She didn't talk much, which made Pete crabby, because he liked to gab. Every time I walked into the kitchen I missed Sophie, and I knew I wasn't the only one.

The pies from the wholesaler had a shiny look when you peeled the plastic wrap off them, like they'd been dipped in nail-polish remover. One after the other, people complained.

"This doesn't taste like the apple pie you usually have here."

"This blueberry pie has no flavor."

"Is your cook using margarine in the crust these days? It used to be so flaky."

I explained that our baker had taken a new job and that these weren't the same old pies that had sprung from beneath Sophie's rolling pin. People were very disappointed, but I told them where they could locate Sophie, so I imagine that bakery in Arlington will get some new customers out of it.

Even I didn't like the pies, and I'll eat just about anything. I made the mistake of mentioning it to Doug one afternoon.

"God, this crust tastes like cardboard," I said.

"Well, don't eat it, then!" he growled. "I'm not paying you to wolf down everything in sight, you know."

"You're in a super mood."

He didn't say anything until I'd made the rounds of the tables with the coffeepot. I perched on the stool behind the register, and he leaned on the counter next to me. "I'm not mad at you, kiddo. It's just I can see the writing on the wall here, and I never liked endings."

"Gus isn't sick again, is he?" I asked.

He shrugged. "He's not sick, but he's not good, either. And losing Sophie, well, I can see it's the beginning of the end. I think we'll stay open through the end of the year, say good-bye to the customers, have one more Christmas season, and that's it."

"Really?"

He nodded.

"Wow. I can't believe it. I miss the place already," I said, looking around at the steamy windows and the carved-up booths.

"Me too. Me too."

And at four o'clock every afternoon, when Lee didn't walk through the front door, I had to fight to keep melancholy from turning into despair. What was going on out there in Indiana, and was Lee ever going to come back here? I missed seeing her sitting in the window, reading her book, sipping tea, waiting for me to finish up. When I walked across the Square past the Brattle Theatre, I saw that the Tennessee Williams festival was over and they were doing a series of Charlie Chaplin movies now. Why hadn't I gone to see *The Glass Menagerie* with Lee? It would have meant a lot to her.

Damn. Everything was falling apart at the same time. Lee had run away from me, the Mug was closing, and Olivia seemed to be nursing her anger too.

She hadn't called me all week, and I hadn't called her,

either. Calling Olivia first seemed like begging, like admitting that I was wrong, which I didn't really think I was. At least, no more wrong than she was. Besides, I was confused. What was I supposed to think about those writing quotations she'd stolen from Mark Twain and T. S. Eliot and all the rest? It was so bizarre—and she hadn't really seemed to feel bad about doing it. She'd said it didn't make any difference to lie to the class because we were all "bozos" anyway. Something like that. Thanks a lot.

But by Friday night I couldn't bear it any longer. I'd see her in class the next morning, of course, but I felt like I had to see her before that, to iron things out, to make it all right again.

She answered the phone on the fourth ring, sounding rushed.

"Marisol," she said. "What a surprise."

A surprise? "You haven't called me this week. Have you been busy?"

"I'm always busy—you know that. I'm not a college kid anymore."

Why did I get the feeling she was *trying* to piss me off? Well, I wasn't going to bite this time. "It's Friday night. We should go out and do something. Dinner, or—"

"I'm low on cash at the moment. I'm throwing together a salad here."

"Well, we could throw together a salad *together*, couldn't we?"

No answer. I persevered.

"I mean, I don't care what we do. We could just walk around the Square or something. I just want to see you—and talk to you."

"We'll see each other in class tomorrow morning." Her voice was clipped.

I didn't get brushed off that easily. "Are you still mad about me going to the Cape with Gio? Or is this about snooping in your computer?"

A heavy sigh rustled through the receiver. "Take your pick, Marisol. I don't like being lied to—you know that."

"But you lied too!"

She sighed. "Oh, Marisol, I really don't have time for this now."

The tears that had been barely contained all week sprang forth. I just couldn't stand being called a liar, especially by Olivia. "I try very hard not to lie to anyone," I said. "Telling the truth—and being told the truth—is the most important thing in the world to me. I never meant to lie to you, and if I did, it was the most benign kind of lie, the kind that protects *you*. I didn't want you to feel bad."

"Are you crying?"

I sniffed. "No."

"You can't even tell me the truth about that! Marisol, I just don't have the time for your dramatics tonight."

"Why not? I thought you were just 'throwing together a salad.' Are you going out again?"

"That's none of your business! I'm sorry. Maybe this is our age difference rearing its head here, but, really, this is just too juvenile for me at the moment. I'll see you in the morning, if you've dried up by then." And the phone went dead.

The shock of her hang-up did indeed dry up my tears. What had just happened here? I was too stunned to move, but my brain was whirling. I needed to talk to someone about this, about *all* of this, but the appropriate friend was not available. Oh, Birdie and Damon were right outside in the living room watching a Steve Martin movie marathon on TV, but I'd already gotten my words of wisdom from them. I felt sure that disturbing them with my tale of woe would only lead to the inevitable "I told you so."

Gio, I thought, might actually be helpful. But it was Friday, the one night of the week he was forced to spend with his father, eating pizza and pretending to "work on their relationship." It usually didn't put him in a sympathetic mood.

This was the kind of thing I could once have talked about with my mother, but since I hadn't let her in on the earlier part of the story, it was too difficult to tell her the whole thing now.

There was nobody I could talk to about any of the important things happening in my life. Nobody I wanted to talk to, really, except Lee, and Lee was gone.

Chapter Twenty-Four

I WALKED INTO THE CLASSROOM on the dot of ten so there wouldn't be time to talk to Olivia; I wasn't currently in the market for any more snubs from her. But I needn't have worried—she barely gave me a glance when I did wander in. I could have been any old slob she barely knew.

I took a seat as far from Olivia as possible and looked around—Gio wasn't there. Just as I was despairing that I'd never find a friend to talk through my problems with, he came running in. "Sorry," he mumbled to Olivia, and grabbed a seat two away from mine.

While Olivia was busy reading some of her favorite first lines from books, I scribbled on a piece of notebook paper, folded it in quarters, and passed it down to him. The two women sitting between us glared at me as if this note-passing proved my immaturity.

The note, of course, asked him to have lunch with me. He read it and nodded his agreement. Thank God. At least someone wanted to talk to me.

Olivia had moved on to having the class read their favorite first lines and then the ones we'd written ourselves. She liked many of them; in fact she was much less critical of this week's work than usual. When Hamilton Hairdo leaned back confidently in his chair and explained that his ridiculous first line was a metaphor, all Olivia said was, "That's interesting. It could work." No, it could *not* work! What *was* the metaphor, anyway? Why was Olivia being so nonjudgmental today? If she thought "The sun reflecting hotly off Albert's cantaloupe-colored head foretold many days of bad weather for the sailors" was a good first sentence, her praise of the rest of us didn't mean much either.

My turn. Olivia nodded, frowning, as I read my first few sentence choices, but when I came to number four, the *Bell Jar* quote, she practically exploded.

"Sylvia Plath! You read Sylvia Plath? That overhyped old suicide? Goodness, I thought you had better taste than that!"

I felt the blood leaving my face and pooling in my stomach. Olivia had once *quoted* Sylvia Plath to me, without crediting her, of course. Now, suddenly, when I quoted her, Sylvia was a cliché? But all I said was, "I like the book, yes. I think it's very good. And the first line . . ."

"Overwritten. Plath never knew when to stop. And so many of the young writers who emulate her are just as bad. Let's hear the sentence you wrote, Marisol." I could practically see her licking her lips over the prospect of chewing my words into pieces.

Was this anger all about me finding the writing quotations on her computer? She obviously wanted to humiliate me in front of the entire class—so much more fun than simply letting me have it when the two of us were alone. There was a part of me longing to stand up and yell at her:

I love you! I let you in! Don't you get that?

But I didn't. I stood up, my voice shaking as I read my first sentence. "'Christina had always believed she was born lucky—smart, funny, and just good-looking enough to get pretty much everything she wanted, except, of course, the thing she longed for most: love.'"

Sure enough, Olivia smiled, then pounced. "Well, that's a mouthful, isn't it? I'm wondering if your book is going to be autobiographical. Because you know, Marisol, the whole world is not interested in the juvenilia of a lovesick teenager. Besides, it doesn't work, does it? It feels manipulative, don't you think, class? Am I right?"

She appealed to her minions, and many heads nodded agreeably, eager to pull me off the pedestal.

"I don't think it's manipulative at all," Gio said. "And what difference does it make who the story is about? Lots of people write coming-of-age stories. J. D. Salinger made a career of it."

"Oh, Marisol's brave defender," Olivia said, waving her hand dismissively at Gio. "I certainly hope no one in here is planning to emulate J. D. Salinger! His time has come and, thankfully, gone! What I want to know is, can't you just write a plain, clear sentence, Marisol?"

What? Like the one about the sailor with the hot cantaloupe head?

The look she sent in my direction was full of rage. It was pretty obvious, at least to me, that this rant had nothing to do with my writing ability. I slapped my notebook closed and stared back at her.

She seemed happy to move on from my juvenilia to the rest of the class's lyrical claptrap. Gio's stuff was good, of course—though Olivia didn't think much of it—and one or two other people could write their way out of a bag, but most of it was pure junk. Which did not stop Olivia from praising its "potential." Talk about lies!

My own anger pulsing in my ears made it just about impossible to listen to anything else Olivia had to say. Obviously, I could never come back to this class again. It was over—the class, my relationship with Olivia, maybe even the whole idea of writing a novel. It had all been ruined by one thing or another.

The minute the class was over, I grabbed my bag and ran for the door, not even looking back to see if Olivia noticed. I was out on Brattle Street, fighting tears, before Gio caught up with me.

"Wait up!"

I slowed down. "I had to get out of there, Gio. She hates me now. My life has turned into a big stinking pile of shit." I wiped away a loose tear, furious at myself for caring so much about someone who didn't give a damn about me, someone who was happy to make a fool of me in front of a roomful of people.

He took my arm and led me down the street. "Let's go somewhere. We'll get coffee and talk."

I was puffing steam like a moose in winter. "Let's go to the Mug. That's one place I'm sure Olivia will never set foot."

"Good. I have something to tell you, and I want you caffeinated before you hear it."

Doug was sitting on a stool at the counter with a stack of

bills in front of him, but he raised his hand and said, "Hey, kiddo," when we walked in. We crawled into a corner booth away from the window. Sue came over to wait on us, her clogs clopping across the floor like horseshoes. "God, I can't believe you come here even when you aren't working," she said.

"Where should I go? *Starbucks*?" I said nastily.

Sue looked to Gio. "*She's* in a mood."

"That's true." He glanced down the page-long menu. "I'd like a tuna fish sandwich and a cup of Earl Grey tea."

"Fries with that?"

"Sure."

"That is so predictable," I griped. "Give me a grilled cheese and a cup of coffee."

"Because *that's* unusual," Sue said dryly, nodding at Gio. "You got your hands full."

Once she left, Gio pulled some papers out of his backpack and spread them on the table.

"Do I really want to know whatever it is you're going to tell me?" I said.

"Probably not, but you have to. Last night, after I finished writing down my first sentences for class, I was goofing around online and decided to look for some quotes. I found these sites last year that list all kinds of famous quotes—I use them in papers for school sometimes, and it impresses the crap out of the teachers. And I thought it would be interesting to search for quotes about writing to put in my next zine issue. So, I'm reading through the quotes—"

"I know," I said, glancing at his sheets of paper.

"You *know*? Since when?"

"Since last Sunday night. I was at Olivia's place, and I went onto her computer while she was in the shower. I know, it was a crappy, sneaky thing to do, but she wouldn't show me anything she'd written, not even a short story. She wouldn't even tell me the first line of her novel, and I was just trying to find *something* . . . and instead I found pages of writing quotations, lots of which she's already used in class."

"Without telling us that somebody else actually said them first!"

"Yeah."

"Is that why she's so mad at you?"

"I guess so. I didn't plan on ratting her out or anything."

"She's really got the art of public humiliation down pat. She must have been embarrassed that you found the list."

I shrugged. "She just acted mad. It was all about my invading her privacy, which I guess I did."

Sue plunked our plates and cups on the table. "You're invading people's privacy now? I'd shoot you."

"Go away," I said. She wrinkled her nose and stalked off.

I stared at the table, where crumbs from somebody else's croissant were still scattered. "The weird thing is, I didn't find much else. There were a few notes for her novel and some ideas for short stories, but no actual writing. Not saved on her computer. And I looked around for discs, too. I can't believe she'd go to so much trouble to hide her novel from me. It's crazy."

We chewed our sandwiches for a few minutes in silence. Gio swirled a French fry in a pool of ketchup and had it halfway to his mouth when the thought struck him. I think the idea was creeping more slowly into my own head, probably because I had more reason to want to keep it out. But there it was.

Gio dropped his fry. "Wait a minute! What if there *is* no novel? No short stories, either. What if she made up her whole career?"

I held my head motionless, hoping the truth would rise to the top. "But wouldn't they have checked her credentials before she started teaching?" Surely there was some excuse not to believe what was becoming clear.

"She was a last-minute replacement, remember? They were probably just glad to get a warm body to show up on Saturday mornings."

"But she teaches at Harvard, too! *They* would check her credentials."

Gio sipped his tea, looking at me sadly. "Do you *know* she teaches at Harvard?" he asked quietly.

I let my head fall into my hands.

"Marisol, I don't think you can trust anything she's told you. Look at the crap she pulled in class this morning. I'll bet she thought you'd figured out her whole nest of lies already, and that was what made her extra crazy."

I held my coffee cup up under my nose so the steam and aroma might twist up my nostrils and soothe my mind a little, so the heat of the cup might penetrate into my ice-cold fingers. I looked across the table at Gio, who could never lie to anyone the way Olivia had lied to me.

I nodded. "You're right. She's lied about everything. Probably including the effusive praise she gave me the first few weeks. Which I was more than happy to believe. God, I'm such an idiot!"

"You aren't an idiot. You may not be quite the genius she portrayed you as, but you're the best writer in the class, and she knows it. That's probably why she liked you to begin with."

"Not my sparkling personality and dry wit?"

"That, too," he said, smiling.

I pushed my mushy sandwich aside; there was no way I was eating food right now. "Gio, I'm so confused. I mean, I loved her. I really thought I loved her."

He looked sympathetic. "I know."

I smacked myself in the head. "God, Gio, did I make you feel like this? I'm so sorry if I did! Did you want to shoot poisoned darts at me?"

"Oh, I wish I'd thought of poisoned darts. Really, Marisol, I felt bad, but there's a big difference here. It wasn't your fault that I fell in love with you; you didn't manipulate me with a bunch of lies. I talked myself into it. And then out of it."

"Can you talk me out of it too?"

"I'll do my best." He cleared his throat. "You, Marisol Guzman, are superior to Olivia Frost in every way. You're an actual writer, for God's sake. She's a big fake!"

I nodded. "Good. Keep going."

"Um, without her makeup, she probably doesn't look half as good."

"Unfortunately, not true. Try a different tack."

"Okay. You are *not* a liar."

"Most of the time," I amended.

"The first line you read today was terrific. I want to read that novel—and if Olivia doesn't, it's her loss."

I sighed. "Ugh, my novel feels dead right now. Like it

got caught in the wreckage or something."

"Are you really going to let her have that much power over you? How much have you written already?"

I shrugged. "Probably a hundred and twenty pages or so."

"Are you kidding? You're halfway there! And you've written a hundred and twenty pages more than Olivia Frost ever wrote!"

That made me smile. "Well, that's probably true."

"Yes, it is!"

"Of course, now I don't have a writing class every week to keep me working."

"I'm not going back there either," Gio said; then his face lit up. "You know what we'll do—we'll have our own writing group on Saturday mornings. Just us two. We don't need her. We can get inspirational quotes off the Internet by ourselves! Maybe Diana could come sometimes too. We can meet here or at a bookstore or . . ."

"Or at my apartment. I can make coffee," I said. "Or even tea!"

"I'll pick up some bagels before I get on the T. There's that place near my dad's apartment."

"Sounds like a plan," I said, feeling better than I had in days.

Gio smiled. "You're going to get over her fast. She wasn't worth your time."

"I hope you're right." We sipped our lukewarm liquids and basked in our friendship, our excellent friendship. "You know who I'd really like to talk to?" I asked him.

"Yeah, I do. Why don't you call her?"

"I don't have her number in Indiana."

"Her sister lives in Cambridge. She'd have it."

"Yeah. But what if Lee's still mad at me?"

"You won't know unless you try."

"Gio," I began, then hesitated.

"What?"

"I kissed her. Lee. I kissed her in Provincetown. Before Olivia showed up."

His eyes went wide. "You did?"

I nodded. "I didn't mean to. I didn't plan it—it just happened. But that made it twice as bad when Olivia appeared."

"Wow."

"Yeah."

After thinking about it for a minute, Gio said, "Lee will forgive you."

"You think so?"

He shrugged. "I don't know, but I hope she does. I really like Lee."

"Yeah, me too."

We sat there quietly for a few more minutes, sipping liquids. It was funny to see the Mug from this vantage point— I'd seldom sat in a booth since I'd started working there. Doug stuck the pile of bills into a brown envelope and took them behind the counter, then started getting the week's laundry—aprons and towels—ready for pickup. Only two other tables were occupied, and those by single people. For a Saturday it was a poor crowd.

The place looked dingy. The linoleum floor was old and cracked, though it was never dirty. The wooden countertop was pocked with scars, the tabletop Formica was discolored by spills, and the curtains in the window were so sun-bleached, you couldn't tell they'd ever had a pattern. Starbucks it was not.

But weren't there still people who'd rather sit in an old booth by a drafty window, a booth where T. S. Eliot might once have had tea, instead of in that crowded chrome coffee palace down the street? Screw Wi-Fi. There was such a thing as authenticity, and the Mug had it. I felt proud to work at the grungiest place in Harvard Square, if only for a few more months.

We left Sue a more generous tip than she deserved, then walked out the door, but almost instantly Gio pulled me back inside the entranceway. "Wait," he said as he stared down the street.

"What?" I said, then peeked out to see what he'd seen. Of course. Olivia Frost, laughing flirtatiously, tossing her locks, headed into Starbucks, her hand wound around the arm of Hamilton Hairdo.

CHAPTER TWENTY-FIVE

"HI. IS THIS LINDSAY O'BRIEN who has a sister named Lee?"

"Yes, it is."

"I, um, met you once at the Arts Festival by the river. My name is Marisol Guzman and—"

"Marisol! I'm so glad you called." I was taken aback by her excitement. Did she have me confused with somebody else?

"You're glad *I* called?" I said.

"Yes! I've been trying to get in touch with you, but your number is unlisted."

"Yeah, my mother makes me do that."

"I'm sure Lee has it, but I didn't want her to know I was getting in touch with you. The thing is I've been talking to Lee . . ."

"Is she coming back soon? I really want to see her and talk to her and . . . I miss her a lot." I wasn't thinking too much about what was issuing from my mouth, but at least I knew it wasn't a lie. As helpful as Gio had been, Lee was the person I really wanted to be with right now, and whatever else that might mean, it certainly meant she was important to me.

"I miss her too," Lindsay said. "I know she'd appreciate hearing from you."

"That's why I called you, to get the number."

"Great, Marisol. That's great. But I also wanted to talk to you about something else. Lee told me about what happened between the two of you, and about your relationship with a woman named Olivia who teaches a creative-writing class."

"That's over," I said. "You don't need to worry about that."

"The thing is . . . I'm sorry if I sound nosy," Lindsay said, "but I'm curious about something. Lee didn't remember Olivia's last name, and I'm wondering if it could be Frost."

I was so shocked, I laughed. "What? How did you know that?"

Lindsay sighed. "Lee described her to me, her looks and her . . . well, the modus operandi fits her."

"You *know* Olivia?"

"She was my freshman roommate at Harvard."

That couldn't be right. I did some quick calculations in my head. Lee had said her sister just graduated from Harvard last year—Olivia was older than that.

"I think you must have her confused with somebody else. This Olivia Frost is twenty-eight years old."

This time Lindsay laughed. "Right. She always did like to add as many years onto her age as she thought she could get away with. She thinks it makes her seem more sophisticated. Believe me, she just turned twenty-three, like me."

I shook my head, even though Lindsay couldn't see me. "I guess I shouldn't be surprised—it's not the only lie she told me. So, she graduated from Harvard with you?"

"Oh, no. Olivia didn't graduate. She got kicked out our junior year for plagiarizing a paper. Lying was her college major."

What? "Oh, my God. What's *wrong* with her? Is every word out of her mouth a lie? She told me she was writing a novel, but I don't think that's true either."

Lindsay sighed. "Everyone who knows her has heard that one. I'm not saying she *couldn't* write a novel—Olivia is very smart—but she never seems to put her energy into anything except her intricate embellishment of the truth."

"Has she ever published *anything*?"

"Not that I know of."

I smacked my hand against the bedroom woodwork so hard it stung. "God, how could I be so dumb?"

"Don't blame yourself, Marisol. Olivia is very good at deception—she's been practicing for years. And she always has an acolyte, someone to adore her, preferably younger, but being an innocent kid right off the farm worked too. I was the first at Harvard, but there were many after me. Men *and* women. And usually more than one at a time."

"Is that what I was too? An acolyte? Somebody to worship her?"

"I don't know, Marisol," Lindsay said gently. "I really don't know."

I was stunned into silence.

"I lost track of her after her expulsion," Lindsay went on. "I thought maybe it had taught her a lesson, but apparently it hasn't. Anyway, when I heard you were dating an older woman named Olivia—and heard about the way she seemed to be manipulating you—I was afraid it might be her. I thought you should know the whole story."

Still, I couldn't speak.

"Marisol, are you okay?" Lindsay asked.

"I'm so sorry," I said, finally.

"What are you sorry for? You didn't do anything."

"I'm sorry that I . . . I didn't see Lee. She was standing right in front of me, and all I could see was that beautiful liar."

Lindsay spoke softly. "I know. Olivia's light is blinding. It's hard to look away."

She gave me Lee's number and apologized again for upsetting me. I assured her I was glad to know everything, but of course that wasn't completely true either. Then we hung up.

I'm not sure why, but I still had that amber necklace around my neck—I guess it's hard to give up on somebody you thought you loved. But the time had come. I took it off and put it into a sock that had lost its partner—which I thought was appropriate—then stuck the sock in the back corner of a drawer. I was pretty sure I'd never wear amber again.

After that I thought feeling sorry for myself might be an option to explore, at least for a little while, and I guess when Birdie and Damon came into the apartment they heard me wailing behind my bedroom door.

"Marisol! What's wrong? Can I come in?" Birdie asked, then burst through the door before I could answer; Damon followed, holding a small white bag. They stood staring at me as I sat on my bed letting the tissues fall at my feet. Noodles and Peaches came in too, bumping against my legs and whining and purring. Thank God for strays.

"What happened? Are you sick? Are you hurt?" Birdie wanted to know as he plopped down on one side of me.

"I never saw you cry before," Damon said, sitting gingerly on the other side. "I don't like it. You're the strong one!"

"Do I always have to be strong?" I said. "I'm having a terrible week, and I think I should be allowed to cry if I want to."

"You cry your heart out, doll-face," Birdie said, giving me a muscly hug. "We're here for you."

I looked at Damon, who was pulling tissues from the box and handing them to me, one by one, a miserable expression on his face.

"How do you two manage it?" I said, sniffling.

"Manage what?"

"Being a couple. You just met each other, and it worked, and that was that!"

"Marisol, you have amnesia! We argue all the time, remember?" Birdie said.

"I know, but you're still together. If anybody had told me that you two would be my role models . . ."

"Hey, some days are good, some days are bad," Birdie said. "This is about that snotty bitch Olivia, isn't it? I can't believe I ever thought she was worth your time. Get rid of her!"

"Too late. She already got rid of me."

Birdie dropped his jaw and popped his eyeballs. "Who does she think she is? Just because she's got a couple of good cheekbones and ten pounds of hair—"

"It's not only Olivia. I feel awful about the way I treated Lee, too. I should have fallen for her instead of Olivia. What's wrong with me?"

"My God, don't tell me Marisol Guzman is an imperfect human being! Sweetie, you were blown *over* by that wench!"

After another few wet minutes, during which Damon rubbed my back and Birdie held my hand, I ran through the litany of the many lies of Olivia Frost.

When I finished, Damon held out the white bag. "Do you want a piece of saltwater taffy?" he asked. "I brought it back from Cape Cod."

I unwrapped a wax-papered piece and stuck it in my mouth. Raspberry. It tasted like our weekend away, and it reminded me I could return to Provincetown another time, and Olivia could never drag me away again. Which was something to hold on to.

"Well, I have no use for that Olivia," Birdie said. "I say good riddance to her. You know, Gio doesn't care for her either."

Damon nodded his head. "Gio says he wishes you could see that Lee is the person for you."

"Wait a minute," I said, speaking with some difficulty around the wad of taffy in my mouth. "The two of you discussed my love life with Gio? That is just plain weird."

"In the car, after we dropped Lee at the airport. Your boyfriends have to look out for you, honey," Birdie said, picking up the damp tissues from the floor with his fingertips and depositing them in the trash.

Finally, I had to laugh at the two of them sitting on either side of me, my fairy godfathers, dispensing tissues and advice, exchanging taffy for tears. Obviously, there *were* people I could count on, some of whom I was just getting to know.

Before Birdie and Damon left, they handed me the phone from the hall.

"Do it now, while you have the nerve," Birdie said.

"And the emotion," Damon added.

"We promise not to eavesdrop."

"We'll turn on the TV so we can't hear."

They tiptoed out, as if my room held a newborn child they didn't want to disturb. I unfolded the piece of paper on which I'd written the number Lindsay O'Brien had given me and punched the numbers into the handset. The phone rang four times before someone picked up.

"Hello?" said a tentative voice.

"Lee, is that you?" I imagined her standing in a hallway, one foot balanced on the ankle of the other, biting her lower lip.

"Is this . . .?" A long pause followed, during which she couldn't seem to say my name.

"It's Marisol."

"I know. We have caller ID."

"Really? Even in Indiana, huh?" My attempt at humor elicited only a nervous noise from her. "So, how are you? Are things going okay with your parents?"

I heard her take a deep breath. "Not too bad. I went online and got some information for them from the PFLAG site, and it helped us start talking. I showed it to my friend Allison, too. She's been over a few times; things are better."

"That's great, Lee. My mother would be so proud."

"Yeah. So why are you calling?" Lee's voice sounded tense, and I wished I could be there next to her, to reassure her I didn't want to hurt her anymore.

"I wanted to talk to the real Lee O'Brien. The Indiana Lee."

"Well, you're talking to her. Did you have something to say?"

No more beating around the bush. "Lee, I'm sorry. I've been acting like a jerk. I don't have a good excuse for it—I just let Olivia take over my brain, I guess. But that's all over now, and if you come back—"

"You aren't with Olivia anymore?" Lee said, interrupting.

"No, not at all. It's a long story. I'll tell you later if you want to hear it, but in the meantime, I think you should come back here. That's why I called, Lee. Please come back."

"Marisol, I can't—"

"Yes, you can! Your sister wants you to come back too. And I need to talk to you. I need to see you. I . . . I miss you!" Once I'd said it out loud, I wanted to say it again and again. *I miss you! I miss you! I miss you!*

"You do?" Lee's voice was almost a whisper.

"Yes!"

She was silent for what seemed like forever.

"Lee? Are you still there?"

Finally, she said, "Marisol, how am I supposed to know what to believe? A week ago you were crazy in love with Olivia; I witnessed it, remember? And now you want me to come back and help you get over her? I don't see what's in it for me."

"That's not why I want you to come back. I want you to come back . . . so we can see what happens next."

"I think I'll just see what happens next in Indiana," she said.

"Please, Lee! The thing with Olivia—she stunned me,

243

that's all. Like one of those spiders that poisons its mate so it can devour it afterward. I didn't even know her—if I was in love, it was with some fantasy in my head."

She gave a little ironic laugh. "Well, you stunned me, too, Marisol. And I'm in no hurry to be devoured again."

"I wouldn't!"

"Do you remember one time I was complaining and you were impatient about it? Instead of whining about life, you thought I should get to work and change the situation. *Fix it*, you said. Well, that's what I'm trying to do. But I have to fix it in Indiana first."

If there was one thing Lee was good at, it was telling the truth.

"So, that's it? You aren't coming back?"

"Not right now I'm not. Who knows? Maybe I'll apply to Harvard for next year, or Boston University, or Emerson, like Birdie."

"But I'll be at Stanford by then!"

"Yeah, I guess you will."

There was a long silence after that. I couldn't convince her, and I couldn't believe it. I guess I really did think I'd been born lucky, that I'd always have a second chance to get what I wanted. But now the thing I wanted most was out of reach.

We each said a final few words, and I clicked the phone off. I was all cried out, but the pain in my chest hurt all the more for being cold and dry. How did people open themselves up to love time after time when it so often ended like this? I understood now why people went to bed when they'd lost love. Because you felt sick, physically sick. What else could you do but sleep until the illness left you alone? I wasn't even sure which emotions I wanted to go away: my insane infatuation with Olivia, or my newly recognized feelings for Lee. They were all mixed up together in a toxic soup that was making my whole body hurt. Maybe Lee was right to stay away from me until I'd gotten them sorted out.

And then I thought: What would Christina do in this situation, if it turned out that Natalie was not who she seemed to be? Or, what if Christina met *another* woman, someone who was not as bold as Natalie, someone she knew she could trust? A woman named Lily, or Lila, or Lydia! I jumped off the bed and opened my computer.

Every Thursday afternoon around four o'clock Christina noticed the same woman walk into the coffee shop across the street from Dr. Hester's office. Why only Thursday afternoons? Christina wondered. And why always that coffee shop, which was an old-fashioned one that didn't even make lattes or cappuccinos? And why did she always dress the same, in a white shirt and black pants? Maybe, *she thought,* this is a silly thing to notice and to wonder about. *Still, she noticed and wondered.*

The day was not over yet. Or the week. Or the semester. Or the year. Things could change. And I had work to do.

Quotations on Writing

123   *"You can't wait for inspiration. You have to go after it with a club."*
    —Jack London

126   *"A writer lives in awe of words for they can be cruel or kind, and they can change their meanings right in front of you. They pick up flavors and odors like butter in a refrigerator."*
    —John Steinbeck

137   *"The role of a writer is not to say what we all can say, but what we are unable to say."*
    —Anais Nin

138   *"It is impossible to discourage the real writers—they don't give a damn what you say, they're going to write."*
    —Sinclair Lewis

204   *"Anxiety is the handmaiden of creativity."* —T. S. Eliot

204   *"If the doctor told me I had six minutes to live, I'd type a little faster."*
    —Isaac Asimov

205   *"When I stop [working], the rest of the day is posthumous. I'm only really alive when I'm writing."*
    —Tennessee Williams

209   *"The difference between the right word and the almost right word is the difference between lightning and a lightning bug."*
    —Mark Twain

209   *"The worst enemy to creativity is self-doubt."*
    —Sylvia Plath